It was one thing to focus on a ghost.
It was another thing entirely
for it to focus on him. . . .

**Other Apple Paperbacks
you will want to read:**

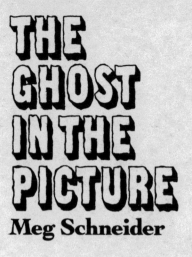

THE GHOST IN THE PICTURE

Meg Schneider

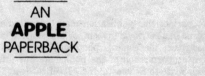

AN
APPLE
PAPERBACK

SCHOLASTIC INC.
New York Toronto London Auckland Sydney

ISBN 0-590-41670-7

12 11 10 9 8 7 6 5 4 3 2 1   8 9/8 0 1 2 3/9

Printed in the U.S.A.   11

First Scholastic printing, November 1988

in memory of my brother
Andy

with love

1

Ben Crisp took one look at the local newspaper and could not believe his good fortune.

He'd certainly had good days before, but this one promised to top them all. Absentmindedly he swallowed another spoonful of oatmeal. It was the chance of a lifetime. Twelve years old, and here it was. His first big break. He couldn't have thought up a better career opportunity. No way.

Just to make sure it was real, Ben read the ad out loud.

"Listen to this, Dad," he began, ignoring the fact that his father was deep in conversation with Stephie, Ben's eight-year-old sister " 'To celebrate the opening of our new Windsor branch, Green State Bank is announcing a student photography contest for best dramatic photograph. The winner and five runners-up will be exhibited during the month of March. Submission deadline: February twenty-first.'

"Do you think it's for real?" Ben couldn't contain his excitement. "Do you?" He began waving the paper in his father's face. "If it is, I'm their man. I know it!"

Mr. Crisp abruptly stopped talking, and with one hand resting gently on Stephie's shoulder he turned to Ben.

"Hey, slow down, Ben. Can't you see I'm talking to your sister? Last night she got into that book of ghost stories we used to have to hide from you, and now she's seeing ghosts everywhere." He paused for a moment and chuckled. "Only unlike you, she couldn't be happier about it. I think she'd send out a welcome wagon if I'd let her."

"But Dad, this is special. This is incredible. *Look!*" Ben started jabbing at the ad with his finger. He hadn't heard a word his father had said. "What do you think? I'm reading it right, aren't I?" The paper was beginning to rip.

Silently Mr. Crisp read the ad, and then let out a sigh. "I should have known this would have something to do with your camera." He shook his head, glancing at Stephie with a mixture of amusement and concern.

Ben grinned. He loved his camera. He had loved it from the moment his father had given it to him. He and that camera were going to be famous. Whatever it took . . . that's what he'd give. One day he'd do the cover of *Life*.

Stephie began to pull at her father's sleeve, her large blue eyes staring at him pleadingly. "Daddy, you didn't finish talking to me. I bet I have seen a ghost. I bet I have. What about when —"

"Stephie, I'm telling you, there are no such things as ghosts," Mr. Crisp insisted quietly and then he nodded understandingly at Ben. "It looks real to me, kiddo. But don't get carried away. You've got schoolwork. In fact," he added, checking his watch, "you'd better get going. You're lucky your mother had to get to the office early this morning. She wouldn't stand for —"

"Okay!" Ben exclaimed, grabbing his books. "I'm outta here." He yanked open the refrigerator, fished out the sandwich he had made for himself the night before, and threw it into his knapsack.

" 'Bye, Stephie," he called out as he ran into the den and tenderly picked up his camera. From now on he was going to carry it with him everywhere. Anything could happen at any time. He had to be ready. He closed his eyes for a moment. Drama. Maybe he'd catch a fire, or a train wreck, or a robbery, or. . . .

3

Ben opened his eyes and checked to see how many pictures he had left. Only four. He smiled as he pocketed a new roll of film. He'd gone crazy snapping pictures at the basketball game the night before. He tried to remember the key moments . . . the dramatic moments. Ben slipped the camera strap around his neck and zipped up his red plaid jacket. Maybe, just maybe, he'd already taken the winning shot. He headed for the front door filled with excitement. Already he could see his work in the bank window.

"Good riddance!" he heard his sister call after him moments before the front door slammed shut. Ben chuckled. She was really a good kid, but eight-year-old sisters could be counted on to understand nothing.

He walked swiftly down the graveled path leading from his front door, but as soon as he reached the sidewalk he stopped. Thoughtfully he ran a hand through his thick brown hair. There was a huge moving van in front of the old Tompson place on the corner. Oh, yeah, Ben said to himself, as he dropped his knapsack on the pavement and hurriedly began to remove his camera from its leather case. Dad said there were people moving in there. He began walking toward the house. It was on the way to school, he assured himself. Well, not exactly. In fact it was in the opposite direction, but only half a block.

Ben brought the camera up to his eye. As the large, old, weathered house came into focus, he could see the crumbling porch and the shingled roof with its battered brick chimney and falling shingles. He focused on the chipped paint that made the clapboard facing look like a mosaic. Ben grimaced, instinctively adjusting the camera controls to bring more light to the dismal image.

"Who, in their right mind, would want to live in that old pile of junk?" he muttered out loud as he stood, as still as could be, finger poised over the shutter, wondering if he should waste a precious picture.

"Me," came the reply. As clear as day. As clear as Ben's view through the lens. He spun around to see a girl about his age with long straggly blonde hair hanging loose over her shoulders. She was almost as tall as he. Actually, he noted with a start, she was exactly *as* tall. Five feet four. She was wearing a light pink ski jacket, jean skirt, and pink high-top sneakers. And she was smiling.

Ben instantly began to fumble with the leather case dangling around his neck. The thing to do was put the camera away. Otherwise he could be arrested as a Peeping Tom or something. Photographers had to watch out for stuff like that.

"No, no," the girl half laughed, as if she could read his mind, which unnerved him no small amount. "That's fine. Be my guest! It's been in our family for three generations. I'm sure my parents would just adore copies. It's not going to look this way forever, of course."

"What do you mean?" Ben asked, casually slipping the camera into its case just the same. He didn't trust strangers. Especially kids his age who said things like "just adore." "What's going to happen to the house?"

"Renovations," she replied mysteriously. "We're ripping some things apart and we're putting other things back together." She laughed, hugging her arms to her chest as if she were hiding something.

Ben didn't like her. He felt as if she were making fun of him.

"Oh," he replied as if he wasn't even slightly interested, which wasn't true.

"My name is Lily," the girl said, extending her hand. Ben thought that was queer. His father did that when he greeted people, but Ben never did. Still it was hard to ignore an extended hand, so he quickly shook it and pulled away.

"I'm Ben," he said once he was a good three

6

feet away. "And I've got to get to school." He headed toward his knapsack which was lying on the pavement behind him.

"Myself as well," Lily replied. "Shall we?"

Ben could not believe his ears. It was the first day of school after Christmas break. It was a big day in sixth grade. He always picked his best friend Jeffers up on big days. That was his habit. His way. Lily was *not* his way.

"I've got to pick up my friend first," Ben answered, allowing an unfriendly edge to creep into his voice. "You go ahead." He didn't feel bad about the way he sounded. She was too pushy. Too strange. Besides, she'd laughed at him. He picked up his bag, hoping desperately she wasn't in his class.

Lily didn't move. She simply stared at him curiously — as if, Ben thought, he were a llama in the zoo.

"Nice to have met you," he tried, hoping to make a clean exit, knowing all the while it would probably be impossible. Lily didn't seem like the type to let a person make a clean exit.

She looked him in the eye. "It wasn't that nice, Ben. Believe me. It really wasn't."

And with that she tossed her long blonde hair over her shoulders and walked past.

Ben stood rooted to the spot as he watched her

7

slight figure heading down the street. "What a pain," he said out loud.

And then for a reason he could not understand, he slipped his camera out of its case, raised his arms, and snapped her picture.

CLICK!

And then he snapped it again. *CLICK!* And once more. *CLICK!*

Ben lowered the camera, a look of bewilderment playing across his face.

Why did I do that? he thought to himself. He watched Lily round the corner and disappear from sight. What was the point of that? Then he shrugged. Must have been artistic instinct, he thought to himself. He looked down at his camera. One shot left. He turned to the beautiful old oak tree across the street, focused, waited for the squirrel on one branch to settle down, and then snapped the picture. It was a nice shot. Not dramatic, but nice.

"Well," he sighed out loud, rewinding the film, "That's the end of that."

Only it wasn't. In fact, it was only the beginning. . . .

2

I'm telling you, Jeffers, this is my big chance." Ben insisted, enjoying the feeling of the camera gently swinging against his chest as he walked. "I'm on my way." He glanced up at his friend, wondering — as always — when he'd be as tall.

Jeffers eyed Ben doubtfully, a stethoscope dangling from his neck. Jeffers' father was a doctor, and he was sure he would be one, too. Or at least some kind of scientist. Jeffers liked facts.

"You don't know you're on your way yet, Ben," Jeffers concluded after much thought. "Slow down."

Ben stared at Jeffers. What was it about this morning? It had started out great at the breakfast table. But already everyone he talked to was getting on his nerves.

Ben could see the school now. "You know, Jeffers," he said, "if everyone took it slow every time they wanted to do something, they probably wouldn't get anywhere."

"That's not true, Ben," Jeffers countered, tossing his straight blond hair out of his eyes. "They'd just get there more slowly."

They walked in silence the rest of the way, and just made it into their sixth grade homeroom as the bell rang.

Ben took his usual seat, turned around to wave to his buddies, and suddenly froze — arm raised perfectly still in midair.

Lily was smiling at him from her seat one row back and three seats over.

"Hello, Ben!" she called out as if they'd known each other forever.

Everyone in the class turned to stare at him. Ben spun around in his seat and cupped his camera case in both hands. It felt nice. Comforting, even. He would have looked up again and smiled at everyone, except he could tell his face was red.

Seconds later Mrs. Simon, much to his relief, took command. "Good morning everyone! And welcome back to school. I hope you all had a wonderful holiday!"

"Oh, we did!" "I went to Florida!" "New Year's Eve was fun!" "My goldfish died!" came the replies.

Mrs. Simon smiled warmly, though Ben noticed

that "let's-get-down-to-business" look creeping across her face.

"Well now," she continued, smiling. "Shall we get down to business?"

No one answered. They never did when she asked that question.

"First of all, we have a new girl in class. Lily, would you like to stand up and introduce yourself?"

Lily stood up and grinned broadly. A few kids began to snicker but she ignored them. For a fleeting moment Ben allowed himself to admire her. She definitely had guts.

"I'm Lily Tompson. My parents and I just moved into the old house on Jasper Lane. It was built by my great-uncle." Lily tucked her hair behind her ears. "Now it's just a big, broken-down house, but we're going to fix it. My father is an architect. In fact, we may put photos of the house in a national magazine."

Mrs. Simon laughed. "Thank you, Lily. Well, we're glad to have you. Aren't we?" She looked around the class and then back at Lily when no one responded to her question. "Have you met any of your classmates yet?"

"I met Ben," Lily proclaimed loudly enough, Ben thought, for the People's Republic of China to hear.

11

Again the class turned and stared at him.

"Well, I'm sure during lunch you'll meet the rest," Mrs. Simon concluded with a smile. "Welcome."

"Now," she said, turning back to the class, hands clasped tightly in front of her, "let's see. We've all been away for two weeks and I bet your minds can do with a little warm-up. Wouldn't you agree?"

Nobody said a word. It was unclear what she was getting at. Ben barely heard her. He was thinking about Lily's house.

"So," suddenly Mrs. Simon reached behind her, grabbed a magazine that had been lying facedown on her desk, and held it aloft. The cover read, *PROGRESS? YES AND NO.*

"Time for a discussion group!" she practically sang out. "Who wants to start? It can be on any subject!" Mrs. Simon's eyes began to dance as she looked around the room.

A few groans seemed to bounce off the walls. Heads began to bow. Eyes turned to the ceiling. Ben had to stifle a laugh. Discussion groups always ended up with someone getting stuck "reporting back to the class." By now most everyone had learned their lesson. No one was talking.

Ben looked down at his camera. He started snapping and unsnapping the case. Under other

12

circumstances he'd have said something about camera technology, but here it wouldn't be fun. Mrs. Simon would ask a lot of questions and before he could say "boo" he'd end up in the library. His mind traveled back to Lily's house. To the national magazine.

Her father is going to need a photographer, he repeated over and over. That's me! Of course it wasn't the exciting first assignment he'd had in mind. Then again, it was hard to find a tidal wave or earthquake in Windsor, Vermont.

Ben tried to imagine the cover of *Architecture Today*. He'd always wanted to have his work in a major magazine. Not that one maybe. But who cared? Ben slipped his camera strap from around his neck, and placed the case before him on the desk. The question was, how could he get the job? Lily was such a pain. And it was such a long shot anyway. He could play all his cards right . . . win her over . . . take great photographs . . . and still not get the assignment. Was it worth the effort?

"Should I take a chance and say something on medical advances?" Jeffers whispered from his seat next to Ben. He placed his stethoscope over his own heart and listened for a moment. "I could pick one horrible disease like bubonic plague and describe how it was treated then and what might happen now, and then I could. . . ."

Ben began to roll his eyes up just as a familiar voice filled the room.

"Well, Mrs. Simon," Lily began. "You know the house I've moved into was built at the turn of the century. And we're slowly going to be changing and restoring it. We'll be adding a new kitchen, but we're putting back the porch . . . or rather a *new* porch that *looks* like the old one. How about that? That's progress, isn't it?"

"Absolutely, Lily! Taking the past and building on it to suit the present is exactly what I mean."

Ben looked down at his desk and gently shook his head. Lily hadn't the faintest idea what she was getting into. He began to scribble absent-mindedly on a notepad. Mrs. Simon was going to keep her busy all semester.

"Why, they're doing it all over the country in urban renewal projects," Mrs. Simon continued. "I think that's wonderful! How about bringing in the old hinges, or nails, or anything else, so we can see how they differ from the new? And I'm sure we'd all love to see pictures of the kitchen and porch in progress. You know, before, during, and after shots!"

Instantly Ben whirled around and looked at Lily. She was frowning. "Shots" were clearly not her thing.

He'd found a way in.

For a moment Ben hesitated. What am I doing? he said to himself. She'll drive me nuts. But then he thought again. He could probably stand her, considering there was a major assignment at stake. After all, taking pictures for the discussion group was only one step away from doing it for the magazine. Who knows, he might even take a shot that was right for the contest! Seconds later, he slipped the camera back around his neck. I'm in business, he decided. Who says you have to like the people you work with?

Ben's mind began to wander. He could see it all now. *CLICK!* A dark, dismal shot of the old kitchen counters. *CLICK!* Counters being ripped out, revealing tangled old pipes and layers of ancient wallpaper. Maybe a scurrying spider. *CLICK!* New counters set into place. Shiny new fixtures and bright enamel knobs. Maybe a plant for extra color. *CLICK!* A sun-filled new kitchen, stew cooking on the stove in a country pot, a digital dishwasher visible in the corner.

Ben looked down at his camera. This was art. This was what he loved most. He could create an entire photographic essay!

He stole a quick glance at Lily. She looked back. He smiled. She didn't.

Ben winced. She had to say yes. Something about this assignment was meant for him. He just knew it.

3

"Pardon me," Lily commented with her mouth half-full. "What are you doing?"

Ben settled into the seat next to hers in the lunchroom. They were all alone at the table. Lily, he noticed, was not doing a great job of meeting people.

"Well . . ." he began self-consciously. "You looked kind of lone — "

"No, that's not it," Lily replied, popping a french fry into her mouth. "You want something."

Ben stared down at his hamburger. This was definitely not going to be easy. Now Lily was sounding like a normal kid. It was eerie, like she was two people in one. He took a bite and chewed slowly. Then he stole a glance at Lily. She was staring at him with piercing blue eyes . . . eyes that said "Don't mess with me, Ben Crisp."

He smiled to himself. He didn't like lying, anyway. It didn't feel good.

"I'd like to be the photographer your father needs," he blurted out, staring at a plaster crack in the ceiling. "For the national magazine."

Lily laughed loudly. "You've got to be kidding! He's hiring a professional for that. I mean, if he wasn't doing that, *I* could take the pictures. I have a camera, too, you know. It may not be as fancy as yours, but — "

"You don't understand," Ben interrupted, a little hurt by her lack of respect for his talents. His experience. "I'm talking really good pictures. I'd develop them myself. I'd use my special lens to zoom in close to details. . . ." He paused a moment. "Also, I could take those pictures Mrs. Simon would like us all to see."

That seemed to do it. Lily looked as if he had gotten through. She smiled at him. Then she looked down at her sandwich, back up at him, and placed her hand gently on his shoulder.

Ben could feel his confidence soaring. He grinned.

"No. I don't think so," she finally said, and then started to stand up.

Ben cringed, quickly looking away. Let her go, he said to himself. No one makes a jerk out of me. Who cares about her dumb house? I'll get another assignment. A better one. He bit into his hamburger. I'll just concentrate on the contest and knock everyone's socks off with my work. Then I'll have my *own* special exhibit. I'll be in a national magazine soon enough.

Lily was now slipping her bag over her shoulder. Ben watched her with complete calm. Who cares about that old porch? What's so exciting about new kitchen fixtures? He could take artistic interior shots anywhere!

Lily began to turn around, and it was right about then that Ben changed his mind.

"Okay! Okay!" Ben hissed through his teeth. "Do you want an apology? I'm sorry. I wasn't very nice to you before. Is that what you want to hear?" He was furious. Ben never liked admitting when he was wrong. Especially to people who didn't take him seriously.

Lily sat down in her seat again. "Actually, yes," she replied.

Ben heaved a sigh. He looked around the room for a moment and spotted Jeffers staring at him. Quickly he looked away. "Okay, can we get together this afternoon after school and talk about when I should come over?" He wanted to meet her father as soon as possible. Gain his trust. Land the assignment.

"No, we can't." Lily took another huge bite of her sandwich. "I've got to practice my figures."

"Math, you mean," Ben half asked, half corrected, thinking he'd never heard anyone say anything so weird in his life.

"Actually, I mean figures," Lily responded calmly. "Figure skating figures. I may be entering a state championship. I want to be as good as I can be. I'm training awfully hard. It's in about three months. Of course, I'm not looking forward to practicing in that old rink. Leo's — right? The rafters are perfect for a bat convention. I can't wait for that new sports arena to open up." Lily put down her sandwich and clasped her hands together, eyes closed. "My trainer tells me I have a real shot at a medal." She looked at Ben. "You and I will just have to start a week from Sunday morning. That's my next free time. Besides, nothing that would be of any interest to you is happening till then."

"Fine," Ben answered, staring at her with surprise. "I play hockey every week. I didn't know you figure skated."

"Well, of course not," Lily snapped. "You're only concerned about my house."

"Look," Ben started to protest, "I told you I was sor —"

"That's quite true," Lily sighed. Thoughtfully

she tucked her blonde hair behind her ears. "Shall we call it a truce?" She held out her hand.

Ben noticed she looked kind of sad. He also noticed that a lot of people were staring at him. He hesitated. Ignore them, he told himself. So it's weird she shakes hands. Says weird things. Big deal. Ben grasped her hand in his.

"Truce," he replied. But he couldn't help himself. He lowered his voice.

"Lily, why do you talk so funny? . . . Like . . . like . . . I don't know . . . like. . . ."

"Grace Kelly," Lily replied without batting an eyelash . . . as if she'd expected the question. She smiled at Ben serenely and tossed her hair back over her shoulders.

"What about Grace Kelly?" Ben tried to remember. He thought he'd seen her in some old movie but he wasn't sure.

"I admire her. She's classy," Lily answered simply. "Did you ever see her in *Rear Window*? You'd like it. She plays this beautiful fashion magazine editor whose boyfriend is a photographer. He thinks he's witnessed a murder through the telescopic lens of his camera and in the end he has to use his camera flash to blind the man who's coming to kill him." She paused for a moment, tilting her head thoughtfully. "I want to be like her someday."

21

"But I thought you wanted to be a figure skater," Ben said, thoroughly confused and a little uncomfortable that Lily wanted to be like someone who had a photographer for a boyfriend. He made a mental note to try and rent the film from the local video store, though.

"Yes, but a classy figure skater. My trainer said I should skate like she acted. Smooth, elegant, and . . . and. . . ." Lily looked up at the ceiling as if to search for the right word. "And cool," she finally added.

Moments later a sad, faraway look filled her eyes. "If it would only come naturally," she added. Then she stood up, smiled a quick goodbye, and began to walk out.

Ben watched her weave her way through the crowded room. So that's what it is, he thought with a knowing smile. He of all people could understand. Lily wanted to be the best, just like he did. No wonder she looked lonely. Sometimes he felt lonely, too.

Moments later Ben stood up to join his friends at a table across the room. I'm lucky, he thought to himself. At least I have friends.

"Got yourself a girlfriend?" Jeffers asked, as soon as Ben took a seat.

"No. I do not have myself a girlfriend," Ben replied with embarrassment, punching his friend's arm with his fist. "I'm going to take the pictures of their house for her father."

"You are!" Jeffers practically shouted. "He actually asked you to take the pictures! I can't believe you didn't tell me that!"

Ben cringed. Everyone at the table was staring at him with admiration. "Well, n-not exactly. . ." he muttered. "First I'm going to just take some pictures for Mrs. Sim. . . ."

The laughter, it seemed to him, was annoyingly loud.

"What is so exciting about that house of hers, anyway?" asked Sam. "Why not photograph the new sports center they're putting up in Greenmount? Now *that's* going to be unbelievable. Talk about progress. You could take some great shots of that, what with all of those huge cranes and everything!"

"Yeah!" everyone concluded, turning to stare at Ben.

"That's true," Ben replied, drumming his fingers on the table. "That's very true," he repeated as if he were seriously considering the idea.

Which he wasn't.

Only he couldn't figure out why.

There was something inside him that was drawn to the Tompson place. It just felt right.

As if he could bring something really special to the job. Something only he could offer.

Ben touched the camera case lightly with his fingertips. He would follow his instincts. It didn't matter if no one understood.

After all, he didn't either.

4

Friday evening Ben sat in his room puzzling
over the contact sheet his father had brought
home from the office. Mr. Crisp was an advertising art director and had brought his son's film in
for processing. Ben checked the envelope to see
if the work had been done at the usual place.
Satisfied, he once again turned to study the glossy
piece of paper where every shot from his last roll
of film appeared in miniature. He shook his head
with disgust. A contact sheet was usually a thrill
to look at.

But not this time.

"I can't believe it," he said out loud with a
pained expression.

Ben brought the sheet up closer to the light, a
look of annoyance playing across his face.

"Please don't let it be the camera again," he
muttered, blindly rummaging around with his left
hand in the top drawer of his desk. Finally he

found what he was looking for. He passed the magnifying glass slowly over three frames. Then back again. "If it's busted again I'll never win that contest. There won't be enough time to. . . ."

Suddenly he heard a gasp from behind him and he whirled around. It was Stephie.

"You want something?" Ben asked irritably, watching her as she gazed down through his magnifying glass at the three pictures he had snapped of Lily walking away.

"I think it's just dust or a scratch on the negative," Ben informed his sister but mostly himself, as he looked back at the funny little smudge next to Lily in the shots. "Or a trick of light." Strange, how it's just on the shots of her and nowhere else, Ben thought to himself. He trained the magnifying glass on the squirrel. Nope. Nothing there. The negatives were downstairs. He'd have to check them later.

Ben looked up at Stephie with mounting annoyance. It didn't seem possible that his camera could be broken again. But, maybe it was. He was sure he'd read the light meter correctly. Ben grimaced. It could be very expensive to fix. He already owed his father for the last problem.

"What are you staring at?" he snapped, lowering the magnifying glass and glaring into Stephie's large blue eyes.

"A ghost . . ." she whispered softly pointing a small finger at the contact sheet. "A ghost next to that girl. . . ." She tucked her long brown hair behind her ears.

Ben burst out laughing. "Steph, come off it. Have you been reading that ghost story collection again? I'm going to tell Mom and Dad to hide it." He couldn't help it, though. Ben picked up his magnifying glass and looked again. Ghost stories had always spooked him. He used to read them and then lie awake all night waiting for some angry spirit to pop out of his closet.

Ben studied the smudge carefully. Dust, or an expensive repair. That was all.

"Look, Steph. There's no such thing as ghosts. Move out of here, okay?" Ben said, walking over to his bedroom door. "I want to take a look at the roll I just shot. I need silence."

Stephie stood up and quietly followed Ben to the door. "Pay attention," she whispered softly. "They usually want something."

"I will," he whispered back with a big-brother patient shake of the head. He closed the door behind her, quickly looked around his room, and laughed again. Stephie's ideas could get pretty wild sometimes.

Ben sat down at his desk, brought the contact sheet up a little closer to the light, and tried to think the problem through. There was definitely a smudge next to Lily. It was kind of a blur, but it was right beside her. It could be dust, only it didn't quite make sense if it was. In each frame it got smaller, just like Lily did as she walked away. It was bigger than her, though. In fact it did look a little like a person. Or rather the shape of a person. And it seemed as if the per. . . .

Suddenly Ben sat bolt upright in his chair. "What am I thinking? I can't believe Steph is getting to me!" He tried to chuckle. He couldn't quite do it. "No way," he continued out loud instead. "Grow up. You're not eight years old anymore. Your life is not the *Twilight Zone*."

Ben leaned back in his chair, and thought hard about Wednesday morning. He hadn't seen a thing. Lily just walked off and left him standing there. He'd focused on her, and quickly snapped three shots. Three shots of Lily and nobody else.

Then again he wasn't perfect. He might have made a mistake — shaken his hand, moved the camera. Ben fiddled with the magnifying glass, twirling it between his fingers. If he was doing something wrong, he had to find out what. So he could improve. So he could be the best. The contest would demand no less.

Ben turned to the shots of the basketball game. He moved the magnifying glass over a picture of

Tall Paul, the school's best forward, making a basket. The picture had energy. It had balance. Drama, even. Ben smiled, suddenly feeling better. This could be a winner.

He was about to push back his chair and go down to his darkroom in the basement, when suddenly his sister's piercing shriek cut through the air.

"Drucilla! She can't come down! What are we going to do?" Stephie pounded up the stairs into her parents' room. "She's so scared! Help! What if she falls?"

Ben ran to his bedroom window and looked out at the tall maple tree that stood across the street. Drucilla, his sister's kitten, was perched on the end of a very thin limb. It was gently waving in the evening breeze, looking as if it could snap at any minute. Things didn't look good for Drucilla.

Ben instantly moved to his bedroom door, but a moment later, he heard his father's heavy footsteps on the stairs. Ben smiled. Things would be okay soon.

Ben reached for his camera. Thinking about first place in the contest, he raced downstairs.

Outside a crowd was beginning to form. Lily was there, standing with two cool-looking adults Ben assumed were her parents. He smiled at her, and began unsnapping his camera case, but Lily looked away. "Very moody," Ben muttered to himself as he gently removed the lens cap from his camera. "Very moody."

"Oh, Drucilla," Stephie began to whimper a few feet away, "Hang on Drucilla. . . ." Anxiously she looked at Ben, but he didn't notice. He could smell a good shot coming. Mr. Crisp had now placed a ladder against the tree. Ben noticed it wasn't very secure. Lily's father and Mrs. Crisp stepped forward to steady it, and Mr. Crisp began to climb. Ben relaxed.

As his father headed up the rungs of the ladder, Ben began snapping. Then he stepped a little closer, and focused on the kitten. *CLICK!* Ben noticed Drucilla was trembling. He wondered if his shot would pick that up. *CLICK!* She'd be down soon. It was going to be fine. *CLICK!*

Moments later Mr. Crisp reached up and Drucilla practically flew onto his shoulder.

"Yay!" everyone down below began calling and clapping. "Yay, Drucilla!" Stephie started prancing around hugging everyone in sight. Except for Ben, who didn't notice.

CLICK! The descent was very important. He'd caught his father going up on the rickety ladder; he had to catch him coming down. *CLICK!*

Suddenly Ben felt a hand on his shoulder. Star-

30

tled he looked up to see Lily staring at him with disgust.

"Ben, don't you think you're being a little selfish?" She tucked her hair behind her ears.

"What do you mean?" Ben was not really surprised that he'd done something she didn't like. Again.

"I mean, this was about your sister and her kitten. Not you and your camera."

"Oh, come on," Ben laughed defensively. "We all knew Dad would get Drucilla down." He laughed again. Louder this time. "Come on!"

"Stephie didn't know," Lily replied softly.

Ben glanced at his sister who was now tearfully cradling Drucilla in her arms. He felt a small pain seize his stomach. Ben looked down at the ground and began digging at a pebble with his toe.

"You are a very unpleasant person." Lily said. "You've got what's important all mixed up."

And for the third time since he'd known her, Ben watched Lily walk away.

"You are not exactly my favorite person, either," he muttered softly, kicking the pebble back and forth between his feet.

Then he turned to approach his sister. But Stephie had already disappeared into the house.

Guiltily Ben trudged upstairs and stopped in

the doorway of her room. Stephie was sitting on the floor rocking a protesting Drucilla in her arms. He hesitated for a second and then walked into his own room, closing the door quietly behind him. He sat down at his desk and looked once again at the tiny photographs of Lily and the smudge.

"Now, why would a ghost want to hang out with you?" he said with a loud chuckle. Then he looked down at his camera with frustration. "Can't you stay fixed for a little while?" he whispered softly.

5

"Ben, it's a fantastic day," Jeffers said, shaking his head as the two of them descended the creaky old steps to the basement Saturday morning. "I don't want to spend it in the dark. . . ."

"It's only for a little while," Ben called back over his shoulder. "It's for the contest, Jeffers. Give me a chance. I want to see how Tall Paul came out." Not to mention check for dust, he thought with a frown. "I play hockey with you, after all, and I'm not so crazy about that."

"Did you know people used to turn purple when they caught the bubonic plague?" Jeffers asked happily, ignoring Ben's comment as he followed Ben into the darkroom. "And that they were just left to die in the streets?"

Ben shrugged his shoulders. "Sounds great," he said absentmindedly. He could already see his winning photograph in the bank's window, and the newspaper clipping underneath.

LOCAL BOY FOCUSES ON THE SPORTS WORLD.
YOUNG BEN CRISP APPEARS TO HAVE AN EYE
FOR WINNING "SHOTS."

Ben grinned. It was a nice pun.

"Well," Ben said as they entered the washroom
he'd converted into a darkroom. "It's time!" He
picked up the envelope of negatives gently in his
hand, and looked at Jeffers, who stood impatiently in the doorway.

"What's eating you?" Ben asked as he began
searching for the negatives with Lily's picture
and the annoying smudge.

"Nothing," Jeffers replied, walking in and closing the door behind him. He placed his stethoscope on Ben's back. "Your heart's beating very
fast. Maybe you need some fresh air."

Ben began to chuckle. "Cut it out, Jeffers. I'm
just worried about my camera." He fished out the
negatives of Lily and held them up to the light,
checking for scratches or dust. Much to his disgust there weren't any.

"Boy," he muttered, "don't tell me it really *is*
the camera." Once again he studied the contact
sheet. Something didn't feel right.

Picking up one negative strip carefully, he
placed it in the old enlarger his uncle had given
him. On the opposite counter he poured three dif-

ferent solutions into three different trays. "Turn off the lights so I don't ruin anything," he called out over his shoulder.

Jeffers flipped off the lights and stood next to Ben as he used the enlarger to adjust the image size. Moments later Ben slipped a piece of photographic paper into the machine and began the process of transferring the image. When the bell went off, Ben turned to the three trays and started soaking the paper.

An image began to appear.

Hardly stirring, Ben and Jeffers stared down at the slowly emerging image. This was Ben's favorite part. The room was dark and quiet. Spooky, even. Just perfect for the magic of it all. He could see the faint outlines of the houses and trees on the street. He could see Lily as she walked away past the mailbox, and Mrs. Field's lawn statue. Slowly it all became clearer, and clearer and clearer . . . except for one spot. Next to Lily.

Jeffers leaned closer, shaking his head. "Who's that? Isn't that Lily? What am I looking at a picture of her for?"

"I wanted to see what that blurry thing was. I thought it was the film, but now I'm afraid it's the camera again," Ben replied. Anxiously he took the photograph out of the tray of developing fluid and placed it in the fixing tray, so that the image would set. He could hear his stomach gurgling. Then he quickly bathed the picture in the wash to get rid of all of the chemicals. Finally he clipped it to an old clothesline he'd strung along one wall of the darkroom, and turned on the lights.

"Is that smoke?" Jeffers asked, pointing to the blur.

"Not sure," Ben replied slowly.

"Fog, maybe," Jeffers tried again.

Ben moved closer, digging his hands deep into his pockets. "Yeah, fog," he answered, only he honestly didn't think it was fog, or smoke. Even his camera seemed hard to blame. Ben moved in closer still, Stephie's words suddenly echoing faintly in his brain. Get hold of yourself, he thought. If she said it was the Loch Ness monster, would you believe that, too?

"Your technique slipping?" Jeffers squinted at the photograph. "It looks like you double-imaged something. Like maybe that's a shot of another guy or something from another picture."

"Of course!" Ben immediately let out a deep breath. How ridiculous. Wasn't it just like him to be spooked so easily? He was simply looking at a double exposure. It didn't really look like one, but then he hadn't studied that many up close. Still. . . .

"Jeffers," he paused, making sure to keep his tone very light. He smiled broadly. "Do you think it looks like a ghost?"

Jeffers began to laugh. He reached for Ben's wrist to take his pulse. "Good sense of humor you got there!" He looked at his watch, still chuckling, and then at Ben's face. Instantly he stopped laughing. "What's with your pulse?"

Ben tried to laugh, but it sounded unreal, so he coughed instead. "I'm kidding," he said, withdrawing his arm from Jeffers' tight grasp. He moved the negative strip over one shot, slipped another harder piece of paper into the enlarger, and set the timer once more. "It's definitely a double exposure," he declared. But no harm checking, a silent voice whispered.

Ben and Jeffers waited quietly, and when the shrill bell filled the air, both of them jumped. Again, Ben began soaking the paper in the developer, while Jeffers leaned against a wall fingering his stethoscope and shaking his head. Ben peered down anxiously as the picture began to take shape. It was there again. It was definitely going to be there again. Finally Ben picked the photograph up, dipped it in the chemicals, and hung it up on the wall next to the first image.

Jeffers picked up the magnifying glass. "Talcum powder," he said with absolute resolve. "She reached into her bag, took out some powder, and blew it into the air." Jeffers placed the glass down on the counter triumphantly. *"Case closed."*

"Maybe so," Ben began slowly with a nod. He noticed the blur still had the shape of a man, but he had to admit it was very hazy. Not quite like a double exposure. Not quite his idea of a ghost, either. All he could see, in truth, was a fuzzy shape. "It sure looked like a ghost, though, didn't it?" He smiled as if he thought the whole situation was very funny.

"No," responded Jeffers. He placed his hand on Ben's forehead.

Ben continued staring at the pictures. "Someone who believed in the possibility of ghosts could really think this was one." He picked up the magnifying glass and held it over the first photo.

"My father is going to have to prescribe a pill for you, Ben." Jeffers started laughing.

"Actually, I'd prefer his season tickets to the hockey game," Ben laughed back, trying very hard to feel good. "I'd rather watch hockey anyday." Then he reached out and gently touched the hazy spots, shaking his head uneasily.

For a piece of dust, or a wisp of smoke, or a cloud of talcum powder, it certainly did look a lot like a man. *But*, he reminded himself, Lily had been all alone that morning. *All alone*. He had seen it with his own eyes. In fact, if not for Stephie the whole idea of a ghost might never have come up. *Never.*

Ben squared his shoulders and looked away. "Let's get outta here," he said, grinning broadly at Jeffers. "It's a terrific day!" Immediately he began putting away the negatives. Enough was enough. Pretty soon he'd start seeing goblins under his bed.

"Hey! What about Tall Paul?" Jeffers asked, as Ben began emptying the chemical trays down the sink.

Ben hesitated. For some reason, Tall Paul didn't interest him anymore.

"I'll catch him later," Ben replied merrily. Even though he had a very strange feeling he never would.

6

We'll just make it," Jeffers commented peevishly, glancing at his watch. "I can't be late like this. I'm captain of the team. It doesn't look good."

"Oh, forget it," Ben answered calmly. "The guys will understand. It's my fault anyway. I made you wait while I finished cleaning up the darkroom." It was the one thing Ben always did on Sunday mornings. It made him feel like a serious professional.

He quickened his step. Leo's Skating Rink was only a block away. They had an hour left before the general Sunday skate session began again. Plenty of time to practice. The others had probably already started warming up.

"You think we'll beat the Ice Hawks next month?" Ben asked, trying to change the subject. "Finally?"

"Oh, sure," Jeffers answered, nodding his head up and down vigorously. "Didn't I tell you? The manager of the Philadelphia Flyers called. They'd like to take us on next. Oh, and did you hear? Olympic scouts are coming to check us out today and — "

"Okay! Okay!" Ben burst out laughing. "I get the picture. So we'll lose again. One day we won't. I can feel it. We just have to keep at it."

Jeffers pulled open the door of Leo's. "Well, next year I think I'm going to take up cycling. It's good aerobic exercise." He shot Ben a glance. "You're welcome to join me." And with that the two of them swung into the cool, cavernous indoor skating arena.

"Hi guys," Ben called out. His teammates were standing quietly around the entrance to the rink, their backs turned toward him. Ben slipped his camera case over his head, sat down on a bench, and not too enthusiastically started to remove his sneakers. He liked hockey, but it didn't hold a candle to his camera. "What's happening?" he continued.

Nobody answered.

"Look, I'm sorry we're late," Ben offered. "It's just that I was cleaning my. . . ." He looked up to finish his sentence, but suddenly realized that

41

no one was listening. Every single one of his teammates were staring out over the rink. Curious, he stood up.

A lone, small figure was skating smoothly and powerfully across the surface of the rink. Suddenly with the gentle sound of blade scraping ice, she was in the air. Then landing. Perfectly.

Dropping his skates on the rubber matting, Ben padded over to the edge of the rink, his eyes wide with disbelief.

It was Lily, and she was incredible.

She could turn, she could spin, she could jump. She could do backward crossovers as easily as Ben could walk. And she was fast. Really fast.

Ben couldn't help it. He started to clap. He could feel his friends turn and look at him as if he were crazy, but he didn't care. She deserved applause.

Moments later Lily skated over with a big smile.

"You like?" she asked in a funny voice. Or, rather, it wasn't so much funny, Ben noted, as it was surprised and kind of shy.

He nodded enthusiastically. When he took a good picture he expected people to say so. It was the same thing, as far as he could see.

"Where'd you learn to skate like that?" Martin

asked, backing away from the ice as if he wouldn't dare go near it anymore.

"Oh, I've been doing this since I was five." Lily grinned. "And I'm not nearly as good as I should be. I don't take it quite seriously enough." She glanced down at her skates. "But I do like to compete."

"Ever break an ankle, or leg or anything?" Jeffers asked. "I mean, isn't there a lot of injury involved in figure skating?"

Lily shrugged. "I suppose so. I've twisted my ankle a few times, and pulled a couple of muscles. Nothing much worse than that." She paused. "Actually I do have a bad knee. Jumping is sometimes a problem."

She looked around at all the curious faces. "Are you gentlemen getting on the ice now? I could work down at the far corner and just practice a few moves over there." She waved majestically toward the far end of the rink.

Ben winced. There she goes again, he thought. Grace Kelly.

"Well, actually, us gentlemen are pretty tired and . . ." Martin began.

Ben heard a few snickers.

"There isn't much time left . . ." Sam finished quickly.

43

"Come to think of it, my ankle still hurts . . ." Max complained.

Suddenly Ben began to crack up and moments later the rest of the Snow Kings joined him.

"We stink," Ben and Sam said at the same time.

"I'm not so bad," Max interjected, rubbing his ankle. "Speak for yourself. It's just that my. . . ."

"You're not so good, either," Jeffers replied. "Bum ankle or not." He started to kneel down on the ground. "Want me to take a look?"

Immediately Max backed away. "It's okay. Later, much later."

For a moment Lily was silent. She looked at Ben with an expression he could only describe as cool.

"Whatever," she murmured and then began to glide backward toward the center of the ice.

For a moment she stood perfectly still and then began to trace figure eights. She was careful, Ben noted, and very precise. Just like he tried to be when he took pictures. He glanced over his shoulder at his camera.

Funny. He hadn't remembered taking it out of the case. But there it was.

Swiftly he walked over, picked it up, and peered through the lens at Lily. He waited. Finally the right moment came. A dramatic moment. Maybe even a contest winner. She was half way through her third revolution, eyes cast down in complete concentration. Her arms and shoulders were perfectly still. Yet the way she held them made them seem as much a part of each turn as her skates. Even her hair, loose as always, swayed gently against her cheeks, echoing the soft curves she was now etching on the ice. Ben pressed the shutter button.

CLICK!

One by one the Snow Kings turned around and shook their heads in his direction.

Ben didn't care. He was used to their attitude. One day they'd understand. When he was famous.

CLICK!

He studied Lily. She was spinning now. Fast. Very fast. Even faster. She was a blur.

Ben smiled. There was definitely more to Lily than met the eye.

Then, suddenly, his smile began to fade. Visions of the three photos he had taken flashed before him. Come off it, Ben scolded himself.

He looked at Lily hard. He looked to her right. He looked to her left. Then he shrugged. She was alone . . . at least as far as he could tell.

7

Tuesday afternoon, Ben swung confidently through the door of Norm's Camera Shop. It felt like a home away from home. There was no one else in the store, and Ben broke into a huge smile. He loved it that way. He and Norm could really talk shop.

"Hey, Norm!" he called out with a wave of his hand. Norm was flipping through files behind the counter. Ben loved calling him Norm. Most of the kids referred to him as Mr. Cohen, but he and Ben had a special relationship. In fact, as a joke, Norm called him Mr. Crisp. Ben liked that.

"Why, Mr. Crisp, how are you, and what can I do for you?" Norm called out cheerfully. He ran his fingers through his unruly dark brown hair. Ben noticed he did that a lot.

Ben slipped his camera from around his neck, placing it, along with a large envelope, on the counter. "I'm fine, which is more than I can say for my camera." He started slowly. "Something funny turned up on some pictures and I thought you could tell me what the problem is." He hesitated. "And soon. You see there's this contest at the bank and I have to get working on. . . ."

Norm closed the files and turned to face Ben. "Yes, sir. I know all about it. Now, talk to me!"

Ben couldn't help but grin broadly. Talking photography was his favorite thing. The whole idea of a ghost seemed more ridiculous than ever.

"Well, I shot a roll of film over the course of a few days. Most of it came out fine, but toward the end of the roll this strange haze kept showing up. I thought maybe the camera lens was dirty. It doesn't look that way to me but maybe you can tell. Of course, I have to say that the haze disappears in the last shot, so I can't figure out whether it's really the camera or —"

"Or a smudge on the negative, or a problem with the film itself, or the development, or one of those odd reflections of light which played tricks with your camera . . . right?" Norm said.

Ben nodded. "Right." Then he looked away. He was annoyed the thought of ghosts was still with him.

"Hmmmm," Norm said thoughtfully, "let's see. Did you have a contact sheet made up?"

Ben nodded.

"And did you see a smudge on that, too?"

Ben nodded again.

"Hmmm," Norm repeated, looking up at the ceiling. "Well, that rules out a mistake with your darkroom equipment."

For the third time Ben nodded. This time with a smile. He hadn't thought it was his mistake, but it was nice to be sure.

"Tell you what," Norm said tapping his fingers on the counter. "I assume the contact sheet and negatives are in this envelope. Yes?"

"You got it," Ben replied happily. Norm was going to figure it out. He could figure anything out when it came to photography.

"Okay, then. You leave this and your camera with me. I'll take a look at everything, maybe even clean up your prize possession a bit and we'll take it from there. Come back in about two hours. I should be done by then."

"Thank you!" Ben practically sang out, as he checked his watch. It was one-thirty. The confusion would soon be over. He was sure of it. No more dust, no more smudges, no more haze, and no more ghosts. *Period.*

Ben waved good-bye, and walked out into the bright sunshine. He turned to his right and started toward the Windsor Bank. Half a block away he could see the hand-lettered sign in the window, advertising the contest. Nervously he stuck both fists deep into his pockets and moved closer.

Moments later, unconsciously, his fingers moved to his chest where his camera usually dangled. Quickly he withdrew his hand and smiled. Always a photographer, he thought to himself. Even without a camera. He studied the sign.

Drama, Ben thought to himself. Windsor was not the town for drama!

He turned away from the window and started toward the video game center. I'll play a few games, he thought to himself. It'll make the time go faster.

But he had only gone a few steps when suddenly he heard the siren. A fire truck was fast approaching. It was still blocks away but the urgent screeching siren filled the air. People everywhere stopped and turned around, eyeing the truck nervously.

"I hope it's not near my home," Ben heard a young man say who had just emerged from White's Haberdashery.

"I wonder if anyone's hurt," another voice from behind him whispered.

Ben paced back and forth. Finally a little drama, he thought to himself, and I don't have my camera. His fingers once again tapped idly against his chest. He wanted the camera so badly he could practically feel it. First place in the contest was only a click away.

"It's Parson's bakery!" a voice called out.

"Is everyone okay?" the young man from the clothing store shouted, hurrying down the street.

"How bad's the fire?" Ben asked, following close behind. Just my luck it will be the biggest fire Windsor ever had, he thought.

"Everyone's out," came the answer. "Fire's not too bad."

"Good," Ben sighed. He turned away relieved. He hadn't missed much.

"Yeah," the young man agreed. He smiled at Ben. "Fires are a terrible thing. Innocent people can go just like that." He snapped his fingers.

For a moment Ben was startled. He looked at the man with surprise, then quickly covered up with an energetic nod. "I agree," he said loudly. "Terrible."

Then he looked away. Terribly ashamed, Ben moved on slowly. Oh, come now, a voice from deep inside him said, you're a photographer. You can smell a good picture. You have to remain objective. Look at news photographers. They have to stay calm. How else would we have gotten such incredible war footage if they hadn't? The fire wasn't *your* fault. You're just doing what a photographer does. Ben relaxed his shoulders. "That's true," he said out loud. "Someone has to keep it together." Feeling lighter, he quickened his step.

Ben opened the door to the game center and walked in. Moments later he was playing.

Promptly at three-thirty, Ben stepped through the door of Norm's Camera Shop. Norm was waiting for him with a big smile.

Ben was relieved. Five weeks wasn't that much time to come up with the winning photo. If the camera was broken he'd probably get it back soon. Norm was the best. Norm could probably fix it quicker than anyone.

"Mr. Crisp! Right on time!" Norm disappeared into a side room and quickly emerged with Ben's camera and envelope.

"Well, I checked everything out. Your camera's clean. I did find a little dust but it couldn't have been responsible for that funny haze in the photograph. And the negative seems clean."

"So, what. . . ?" Ben felt the unease he'd been fighting most of the week begin to take over.

"Well, it's either a flaw in the roll of film, a flaw in the processing of that film, or just one of those hard-to-predict problems with light reflection. Was it a sunny morning when you took those pictures?"

Ben nodded.

Norm nodded his head. "Look, your equipment seems fine. It was probably just one of those things. Enjoy yourself. Forget about it."

Just a little unnerved, though he tried to shake it off, Ben slipped the camera around his neck and tucked the envelope under his arm. "All right," he said. Norm knows what he's talking about, he thought to himself as he stared down at his camera. Forget about it.

He looked up at Norm and smiled broadly. "I'm going to take your advice."

Norm nodded. "Good idea. By the way, Ben," he added, his eyes twinkling, "there is one other possibility. . . ."

Ben's heart skipped a beat. Good-bye spirit world, he said to himself. Hello earth.

"Have you considered ghosts?" Norm asked, chuckling loudly.

Ben just stared.

"Hey, Ben . . ." Norm said, resting his hand on Ben's shoulder. He wasn't laughing anymore. "I'm just kidding. But the truth is too much light coming through the lens can produce ghostlike streaks." He paused. "But it's not a ghost. Trust me. A bad joke maybe, but no ghost."

Ben nodded, and managed a weak smile. "I know that," he practically whispered. And then, without saying another word he turned on his heels and walked out the door into the bright sunshine. He was almost all the way home before he was able to find his sense of humor again.

"Yuk, yuk," Ben said, as he went up the walk to his front door.

Trouble was, nothing had ever seemed less funny to Ben in his whole, entire life.

8

Thursday evening, Ben felt as if he'd walked into a long black tunnel that had no exit at the other end. It was just too weird.

He stared down at the new contact sheets, training his magnifying glass over the shots of Lily scratching figure eights in the ice. A faint rattling sound suddenly seemed to fill the room and with a frightened start he realized it was only the sound of his own uneven breath. His eyes returned to the contact sheet before him.

Once again, Lily was not alone.

Ben reached for the phone.

"Jeffers," he began slowly, trying to keep his voice steady. "You won't believe this, but remember those photos I took of Lily the —"

"Oh, Ben, listen," Jeffers interrupted. "I've been thinking. This may be crazy, but as captain of the team I think it would be a good idea to see if Lily would like to give our team some pointers on — "

"*Jeffers, listen to me!*" Ben practically shouted. Get hold of yourself, a voice from deep inside implored. You're getting all worked up about nothing. It's probably nothing.

"Okay, okay," Jeffers snapped. "Boy, what's eating you?"

"Jeffers, I think something really weird is going on. I mean, remember those pictures I took of Lily at the rink the other day?"

"Ben . . ." Jeffers chuckled, "You're not going to start again with that business about. . . ."

Out of the corner of his eye, Ben saw his door open a crack, but he couldn't help himself. He had to keep going. He had to get it out.

"It's there again, Jeffers. It's there. It's not any clearer than the other pictures, but it's there again."

For a moment Jeffers was quiet. Ben waited. He wished he could explain things more clearly, but there was no point trying. He knew the words wouldn't come.

Ben turned around. Stephie was standing in the doorway. Impatiently he waved her away, but she didn't budge.

"Look, the lighting in that place is horrible,"

Jeffers finally began. "Also, it's cold. She was probably breathing out warm air and it made a little vaporized cloud next to her. That always happens when people are in a cold place. Think about it. I mean. . . ."

Ben sat up straight. Of course. Jeffers was right. What's the matter with me? It could easily be that. He was beginning to feel like a fool.

"Oh, yeah," Ben replied. "That's probably it." He breathed a deep sigh of relief, holding the magnifying glass over one of the frames. It was true. It could have just been exhaled breath. A lot of it. But breath just the same. "Thanks, Jeffers. You must really think I'm losing my. . . ."

He passed the magnifying glass over the second shot, and then the third. Suddenly his hand started to quiver.

"Jeffers," Ben rasped. "If a person is standing still in a cold room and he breathes out, the smoky-looking breath is going to be in front of his face. Right?"

"Unless his mouth is under his ear," Jeffers replied with growing impatience. "What kind of a stupid question is that?"

"I have a picture of Lily standing perfectly still, facing the camera, but that smoky blur is to her left!" Ben blurted out. *"How can that be?"*

Ben could sense Stephie standing behind him

now, excitedly leaning over his shoulder. She was practically jumping up and down.

"Maybe someone opened the door to the rink and the wind blew it!" Jeffers shouted back. *"How should I know?"* He paused. "Look Ben, I don't know what's going on with you and this ghost thing but you just don't have any evidence. All you have are a bunch of cloudy photographs. I mean, I'd like to help you, pal, but I can't. I don't believe in ghosts. When you're dead, you're dead." He paused a moment. "Wow, Ben. Does this have to do with the contest? Are you trying to take a picture of a ghost to win that contest? Because if you are I'd say you have really cracked your — "

"It has nothing to do with the contest." Ben tried to force out a chuckle. Once again he had to turn it into a cough. "But I guess you're right. It must have been a cloud of frozen breath." Debating phantoms with Jeffers was getting him nowhere.

"I am," Jeffers replied, clearly ready to put the matter behind him. "I'm also right about Lily. What do you say?"

"About what?" Ben asked, not really listening. He held the magnifying glass over the third picture.

"About getting her to give us some pointers. I

mean, no offense, Ben, but you turn on the ice with the speed of a five-hundred-pound gorilla."

Ben laughed in spite of himself. It felt good. "Well, skating like a five-hundred-pound gorilla is better than skating like a caterpillar. By the time you make it across the full length of the rink the game's over."

"Whatever you say," Jeffers replied good-humoredly. "But will you ask her? You know her better than we do."

"Sure," Ben nodded. "As soon as I get a chance. But I don't think the rest of the guys are going to go for this at all."

"Leave them to me," Jeffers answered confidently. "You just get Lily. And Ben," he paused, chuckling loudly, "tell her to leave her friend home. Okay?"

"Sure!" Ben answered as if he hadn't a care in the world. Then, just to sound convincing, he added, "You bet!"

The moment he hung up, Ben's smile disappeared. He held the contact sheet up to the light. Exhaled breath, it seemed to him, had nothing to do with it.

"Wh . . . what . . . is it?" a soft, small voice seemed to float about the room. Ben turned around slowly and looked into Stephie's wide blue eyes. For a moment he almost told her exactly what he was thinking.

"Go back to your room," he finally said, instead. "Please, Steph. I have to study. It's nothing." He turned to his desk and flipped open his book on the Civil War. Stephie would only confuse things. Spook him even more. Make him see things where there was nothing to see. Ben grimaced. Come to think of it maybe she'd done that already.

Stephie didn't move, but Ben stubbornly refused to look up again.

"It's a ghost, Ben," Stephie said very slowly. "I know it."

"Hey Steph," Ben snapped, "I don't need this from you. Keep it to yourself."

"But maybe he's trying to protect Lily. Tell her something. Maybe even warn her about something. You have to tell her!" It seemed to Ben that every inch of Stephie's body was vibrating with excitement.

Ben gave her a long, hard look. "Stephie," he said, "aren't you just the slightest bit nervous or upset about this?"

"Why?" Stephie suddenly stopped moving. "It's not standing next to me, is it?" Quickly she looked to either side. Satisfied she was alone, Stephie placed her hands on her hips. "Ghosts are cool. I don't believe most of those horrible stories. I think they probably just do mean things if they're angry at you when they're alive, or if you bother them once they're dead."

"Oh, really?" said Ben. "How'd you learn all this? Interviewed a ghost lately?"

Stephie was thoughtful. "I don't think so, but once I —"

"*Out!*" Ben cried. "*Out!*"

Her eyes sparkling with pleasure, Stephie turned around and walked toward the door. "I'll disappear Ben, but I think I'm the only thing around here that will." And with that she was gone.

Ben closed his textbook, turned off his desk light and bending over, rested his head in his arms. His mind began to spin as he played over and over the events of the last few days, searching for a clue to tell him what it all meant. What he was supposed to do. Whether or not he was losing his mind.

But it wasn't until he was lying in bed late that night that Jeffers' words came back to him . . . and the idea began to form. At first it seemed terrifying — too terrifying, in fact, to even consider. But the more he thought about it the less frightened and the more excited he became.

If it is a ghost, Ben reasoned, and it may not

be, but *if* it is, what could be more dramatic? Who else could capture a ghost on film for that contest? Ben could see the newspaper clipping:

LOCAL BOY FOCUSES ON THE SPIRIT WORLD.
IS IT OR ISN'T IT?
YOUNG BEN CRISP HAS GIVEN US SOMETHING
TO THINK ABOUT.

Suddenly Ben shivered. There was only one problem, and it was inching its icy way up Ben's neck.

What if it really was a ghost? What if he took an even better picture next time? A clearer picture? And what if that ghost didn't like it one, little bit? What if, as Stephie said, he bothered a ghost?

Ben pulled the down comforter up to his neck, trying to feel warm. It didn't make any difference. He was shivering all over. Seconds later he jumped out of bed, pulled a wool blanket from the closet, wrapped it around himself, and got back under the comforter.

It helped. But only a little.

9

T hat's Pete," Lily said, nodding toward the biggest man Ben had ever seen in his life. "He's our construction person."

Ben couldn't help himself. He brought the camera up to his eye and snapped a picture of Pete as he lifted a huge plank of wood over his head. The guy had muscles up to his ears.

"Are you planning to use that shot during the discussion group?" Lily laughed, as she led Ben from the front door into the living room. Gracefully tucking one foot behind her, Lily gently lowered herself onto the old wood floor. "By the way, my father is using a photographer from the magazine." Lily glanced up at Ben for only a second and then began tracing a circle on the wood floor with her finger. Ben wasn't sure, but he had a feeling Lily was genuinely sorry. He wanted to tell her it was okay. That he had other things on his mind now. But the words wouldn't come.

"Shall we decide how we're going to proceed?" Lily asked brightly, finally looking up again.

"Well," Ben began, quickly letting his eyes glance at the empty spaces on her right and left. There was nothing there. "We could start with the outside . . . or we could start downstairs, move up and then do the outside." Ben shrugged. "I don't care. It's your house." And your ghost, he thought to himself ruefully. Ben looked around Lily's house and started having second thoughts. Everything was a mess. He'd started out hoping for a major magazine assignment and now he was stuck taking pictures for Mrs. Simon and ghost hunting. It was all too pathetic to believe.

Maybe, Ben thought to himself, I should just go home. I'll say my camera is broken and call it a day. Thoroughly convinced it was time to leave, Ben was about to say so, when visions of the bank window flashed before his eyes. He hesitated.

Suddenly Lily was on her feet. "I need a sweater. Just wait here," she said as she headed for the hallway.

"But it's warm in here!" Ben called after her. "For that matter, it's warm outside! It's fifty degrees!"

Lily walked back in, pulling on a thick red sweater. "I know it's warm," she shrugged. "But I can't help it. Sometimes I'm in the house and I feel a sort of chill sweep by me. There must be cracks in the walls or something."

Or something is right, Ben thought to himself.

"Hello, Ben!" Mrs. Tompson called out as she rushed through the front door. "This place is wild now, isn't it?" She started dropping shopping bags filled with nails, paint, and shelf covering all over the floor. "Whew!" she laughed. "And this is just for one bathroom!"

"Mom, is it all right if we wander about the house? We won't be in anyone's way, will we?" Lily asked. She clasped her hands in front of her.

"No, Grace," her mother replied with an affectionate smile. "Pete's not going to care, and neither should the people working for him upstairs. Just don't bother them." And with that she started out the door again. "Tell your father I'll be right back. I forgot a few things. Oh, and by the way, I picked up *To Catch a Thief* at the video store. You'll have to return it yourself tomorrow." The door slammed shut behind her.

"What's that about a thief?" Ben asked, looking at Lily curiously.

"*To Catch a Thief,*" Lily corrected. "A fabulous Grace Kelly movie." Her eyes traveled to the ceiling. "She's *sooo* beautiful in that movie. *Sooo* elegant."

Ben coughed uncomfortably as Lily continued

to gaze upward. Her weirdness was getting on his nerves again.

"So," she finally began, much to his relief, "What shall we do first?"

Ben sighed. It felt like Lily was "shalling" him to death. For a fleeting moment he understood why his camera sometimes drove his friends crazy.

Ben looked around the living room and spotted an old, filthy fireplace. "What about there?" he pointed. "You guys going to fix that?"

"Well, not exactly," Lily frowned. "My mother wanted to, but my father is planning to put in a new potbellied stove because it gives off a lot of heat. That way the bills won't be so high."

"Well," Ben paused. "Potbellied stoves aren't exactly progress. Then again, I bet it's okay to show how old stuff can really be the best thing!" He focused. *CLICK!*

"Here, look at these," Lily waved Ben over to the windows. "You see all this chipped wood?" she said, pointing at the sills. "Well, these are all coming out and we're putting in new windows." She smiled proudly. "That's definitely an improvement."

"Okay," Ben said unenthusiastically, as he stepped back to take a picture. Lily started to move out of his way. "That's all right," Ben said quickly, motioning her back into the frame. He couldn't help himself. He had to see. "It's your house."

Lily smiled into the camera, one hand resting on the sill. Then, a second later she shivered. Quickly she stepped away from the window.

Ben stared at her in amazement. The window was tightly closed. And he was about to tell her so when his eyes traveled to a dusty portrait which was leaning against the wall, half hidden by the old curtain.

Lily followed his gaze. "Oh, that's my great-uncle. He's the one who originally built this house." She chuckled, pushing back the tattered curtain. "I'm afraid, speaking of progress, he didn't get very far. He was killed mountain climbing when he was a young man."

Ben stared at the painting. The man looked very tall and athletic. A heavy rope hung around his shoulder. Ben's mind flashed back to the blur. Nah, a voice inside him whispered. Don't even think it. Still, Ben wished he'd brought the photographs with him to compare. Then again, he thought, looking at Lily, he didn't want to give her any more chances to make a fool of him.

"What happened to your great-uncle?" Ben asked, both hands clutching his camera. He stared at the portrait. It looked alive. It was staring back. Stop it! Ben scolded himself.

"Well, the story goes that he was with a guide somewhere in the Alps and he walked off by himself without any equipment. Not even an ice pick or rope. He slipped on some ice and the guide just couldn't get to him in time. He plunged into the crevasse. Something like that. Anyway," Lily added, looking at the painting, "I do know his last words as he plunged headlong into the abyss. . . ."

Ben quickly glanced at her. She was actually enjoying the story. Her eyes were gleaming.

"He said, *'The rope! The rope!'* " Both hands went to her hips. Lily smiled at her great-uncle proudly. "You see, the guide tried to throw it to him. My great-uncle got one hand around it and held on for as long as he could, but suddenly it just slipped away." She stepped toward the painting and ran her finger along the edge of the frame.

And then Ben felt it. It was gentle. Very gentle. But it was there. It was as if something had him by the arms, and was moving him about. Making him do things. And the thing he was doing was bringing his camera to his eye, focusing, and snapping a picture of Lily. Her back was to him. But he couldn't seem to stop himself.

CLICK!

Lily whirled around. "What did you take a picture of? Him?" she asked with surprise. "Why are you bothering to. . . ."

Ben *had* to ask her. It was bursting out of him. But just to be safe, he planted a big broad smile on his face. Then he willed his heart to stop pounding in his chest. Finally he spoke.

"Lily, do you believe in ghosts?" he asked. The smile was already hurting his face.

"Are you kidding?" Lily laughed. "I certainly do not. That's for little kids! Why? You don't — "

Suddenly Pete walked into the room. "Gotta measure some shelves, kids," he boomed.

"I thought you did that already," Lily answered, quickly walking over to inspect the plans he was carrying in his hand.

Grateful for the interruption, Ben walked out, leaving Lily behind. He had a feeling if she'd kept talking, he'd have felt as small as an ant.

"Wow, Pete, those shelves are going to look great," he heard her say. Good, Ben thought to himself as he wandered into the dining room and sat down on an old cane chair. He needed to think. Ben closed his eyes.

I'm not scared, he informed himself, which was true. He wasn't. He had been, but he wasn't now.

Ben thought about that. Whatever it is, he said to himself, I don't think it's out to get me. He opened his eyes and looked around just to be sure.

"Are you here?" he whispered.

Nothing happened. Ben stood up and circled the room. "What do you want?" he whispered again, very softly. "Do you want me to take your picture? Is that it?"

Again, nothing happened. He could hear Lily chatting with Pete, and the banging upstairs, and the cars driving by, but nothing, absolutely nothing, from the spirit world.

Ben sat down again. Okay, he said to himself. This is it. You have to decide. Is this really going on or are you just letting your imagination go crazy? Which is it? And if it is going on do you want to get involved?

He waited for the Jeffers side of him to answer. The part that could find the facts. He waited . . . and waited. But there was silence. Ben looked down at his camera. "What are you seeing?" he whispered. "What are you trying to tell me?" He gently wiped the lens off with his shirt cuff. "Are you trying to help me get a better picture so I can win that contest?"

Suddenly he heard a voice behind him. "Hey, kid. You seen my rope anywhere?"

Ben whirled around wide-eyed, half expecting to see Lily's great-uncle. But it was only one of the workers from upstairs.

"N . . . no . . ." he stammered, trying to pull himself together. He stared at the tall, grubby-looking man standing in front of him.

"I don't know where it went," the man muttered. "Can't figure it out for the life of me. . . ." And then he disappeared.

Ben sat quietly in the dining room for a few minutes. His camera hanging from his neck lay nestled in his lap.

"Ben!" a voice pierced the air. "Where are you? We have to get to work!"

Reluctantly Ben pushed his chair back from the old table and started to stand up.

Only he didn't get very far.

Suddenly the chair began to topple backward. Ben felt himself falling in slow motion, and what seemed like minutes later he lay sprawled on his back on the dining room floor.

For a few moments he just lay there, stunned. Then, shakily, he slowly got to his feet. He was about to pull the chair upright, when he saw it.

The rope.

It was tangled in the feet of the chair. It was thick. Very strong-looking. And it lay there, as if, Ben thought, it were waiting for him. It seemed to whisper, *"Pick me up."* He looked around wondering if he should call after the workman. "Hey, I found your rope!" he wanted to shout.

But in his gut, Ben knew better. It was not his imagination. The feeling was too intense for that. Confused, he bent down, picked up the rope, and dangled it over his shoulder. Like in the portrait. "That's right," a voice murmured from somewhere. Ben started. It had been his voice, but it had seemed to come from another place. Another person.

"There you are!" Lily announced, practically skipping into the room. "Let's go!" She grabbed Ben by the arm and pulled him into the hallway. "Why the rope?" she flung over her shoulder, clearly not too interested. He didn't answer, hoping she'd just throw herself into a tour of the house, which is exactly what she did.

They began on the first floor. Ben didn't let on a thing. They inspected the bathroom pipes, the closets, the doorknobs, the moldings, and the wood nails. Sometimes Ben took pictures, other times he was so lost in thought he forgot. Do I want it to be a ghost? he asked himself over and over. Is that why this is happening? So I can try to win that contest? His fingers lightly touched the rope. Could this all be in my mind?

Finally it was noon. Lily checked her watch. "Time for figures," she said. "I've got to eat something," she added.

Ben followed her out of the sun porch and back to the front door. He looked over his shoulder into the dining room. It seemed like an ordinary room now with the chair tucked back under the table.

Standing at the front door, Ben almost told Lily everything, even though he was sure she'd laugh. Very hard. And at him. He had a creepy feeling that she *ought* to know. That this wasn't just between him and his camera. That she was involved, too. But he couldn't figure out how to tell her. What could he prove? And would she let him keep going for the sake of the contest? Why should she? It was her ghost. Then Ben thought of his darkroom . . . the hours he'd put in there. The possibility that if it really was a ghost, and it wasn't after him, and it was practically posing. . . .

It was after all, Ben decided, his ghost, too.

The words BEN CRISP — FIRST PRIZE danced before his eyes.

Something told him not to let on.

"Well," he said patting his camera, "I think we did pretty well today, Lily. We should do this same thing next Sunday."

"Or maybe one evening this week," Lily offered. "We don't want to miss anything important around here."

Ben half grinned and half grimaced. "Yeah, okay," he said. And before she could say another word and Ben could think another thought he snapped her picture. *CLICK!*

"What did you do that for?" Lily asked. "You're wasting film."

Ben shoved his hands into his pockets in an effort to hide the fact that they were shaking just a little bit. He'd felt something lift his arms again.

"There's only a couple of pictures left on this roll of film. I want to use them up," he lied. He started walking down the rickety front steps and then suddenly remembered Jeffers' suggestion.

"Oh, by the way," Ben called out, turning around once more. "Lily . . ." he looked down at his sneakers. Somehow it didn't seem right asking for a favor. "We were wondering if you could give our hockey team some skating pointers." He kept looking down, sure she was going to laugh . . . tell him the Snow Kings could lose every game from here to eternity as far as she was concerned. He wouldn't have blamed her.

But he was greeted only with silence. Dead silence.

Finally he looked up to see Lily staring at him with an expression of complete happiness dancing across her face. He'd never seen her look that way before. It made her look different. Nice, even.

"Why, I'd just adore that," she answered softly. "Really, I would!"

"G . . . good," Ben answered, looking away once more. It was embarrassing. Please, he thought to himself. Whatever you do, Lily, leave Grace home. "We'll figure out when later," he continued.

"Fine," Lily smiled warmly. "Oh, Ben, aren't you forgetting something? Isn't that our rope?"

Ben couldn't move. He was sure he was meant to keep it. Absolutely sure. Why was this happening? His mind began to race.

"I . . . I need it for artistic purposes," he lied. "I need it to get up high enough in the trees to photograph your house from the outside, too." Then he waited. He hadn't made a lot of sense but it was the best he could do with no advance warning.

Lily nodded. "Yes, I know how it is with art. Skating is very artistic, too. Go ahead. Take it."

Ben smiled as if he never doubted her permission and then swiftly turned around. He was so tense he wanted to scream. Taking a long deep breath he looked at his watch. Jeffers, Sam, and the other guys would be waiting for him at the lake. It was time for their weekly hockey game.

Reaching the sidewalk he turned and looked at the old Tompson place. He fingered the heavy rope on his shoulder.

Then, he looked down at the leather case dangling from his neck. Suddenly he was afraid to touch it.

10

I cannot believe you are still talking about this,"
Jeffers chuckled as he warmed up on the ice
of the lake. "I thought I'd straightened you out
on the whole ghost business. *Breath or dust!*
Remember?"

"So what about my arms being lifted?" Ben shot
back, turning sloppily on his blades to a backward
glide. "What about that?"

"It's in your mind, Ben," Jeffers insisted. "You
wouldn't believe how much your mind can affect
your body! My dad's always saying that half the
problems his patients come in with are all — "

"I'm not one of your father's patients," Ben returned with growing annoyance. "And besides,
what about the rope?"

"What about the rope? I mean, it's not like the
rope appeared from nowhere. It was lost. The
guy was looking for it. It happened to be under

your chair! If you'd found a yo-yo would you have thought the ghost left that for you also?" Jeffers shook his head. "I don't know Ben. I'm really surprised at you."

"Drop the puck," Ben snapped. "Let's shoot it around until the guys get here."

Shrugging, Jeffers reached into his pocket and dropped the heavy black disk onto the ice. Silently they began passing it between them.

Maybe he's right, Ben thought to himself. Maybe I am making this whole thing up. Maybe I want to win that contest so badly I'll do anything, think anything. He glanced at Jeffers. No. It's a ghost, there's no other. . . .

"Hey! Pay attention!" Jeffers yelled out, as the puck whizzed by Ben's motionless stick.

Ben flashed him an apologetic smile. "Sorry. Let's go," he said, but his heart wasn't in it. He was too busy thinking. It had to be a ghost, which was creepy but okay. There wasn't a bone in his body that told him it meant to hurt anybody. Ben wondered if he could convince the ghost to make itself a little clearer . . . a little easier to pick up with the camera. He looked at Jeffers. First place in the contest was so close he could smell it. Keep laughing, he said to himself. I'll show. . . .

What am I saying?! Ben suddenly started.

77

Ghosts don't come back for no reason. The books say they always come back for unfinished business. Didn't Stephie say they only appear when they want something? How can I be thinking about the contest at a time like this?

But Ben *was* thinking about it. In fact he was thinking about it so hard he didn't notice the large rock in his path.

Moments later, for the second time that day he lay sprawled on his back in complete surprise.

"What happened?" Jeffers called out.

"Nice goin'!" Ben heard laughing voices from the left side of the lake. The other players had arrived.

Ben cringed. Gently he eased himself onto all fours. Jeffers reached out and offered him his hand, but Ben ignored it. He felt like a fool. The least he could do was get to his feet by himself. He steadied himself, then, staring down at the ice, he saw the crack.

It wasn't very big. But it was big enough.

"Look," Ben said softly, as if he thought saying it quietly would keep the lake from knowing.

Jeffers stared. "It . . . it doesn't look too bad," he said hesitantly. He studied the shoreline trying to figure how far they were from safety. He looked at the crack again. "I don't think it's spreading, either. The ice is still too thick. It must have happened when you fell."

Ben started to stand.

"*No!*" Jeffers practically screamed. "Don't put any pressure on that spot." He started to back off slowly. "In fact, don't put too much pressure anywhere. Sit down on the ice and slowly push yourself a few feet to your right. I'll follow you."

Ben sat back down on the ice and carefully began to move. The crack did not get worse.

Moments later he scrambled to his feet, and with his heart in his mouth he quickly skated over to his friends, Jeffers several feet ahead of him all the way.

"What was goin' on out there?" Sam asked, tying a double knot on his left skate. "Ben, you decided you needed a rest?"

"Forget skating today," Jeffers announced impatiently, throwing himself down on the ground and picking at his laces. "It's been too warm for the last few weeks. The ice isn't thick enough."

"That's crazy!" James called out. "I was skating here yesterday with my brother. It was fine!"

"Well, it's not so fine in the center of the lake," Jeffers answered sharply. "If you wanna skate go ahead. But you can count me out."

"Me, too," murmured Ben. He looked out onto

the ice. The surface seemed to shimmer as it reflected the sun's piercingly bright rays, yet the lake still looked very cold. Very cold and very unfriendly.

"Earth to Ben, Earth to Ben," Sam intoned as he waved his hand in front of Ben's face. "What is it with you?"

"Wh . . . what?" Ben replied, trying to focus on his friend. His eyes wandered out over the lake again. It was so still . . . as if it was waiting . . . waiting to reveal a secret that lay deep down underneath the ice.

"Jeffers, is this Ben here really an alien pea pod?" Max laughed, nudging Jeffers.

"Okay! Okay!" Ben smiled. "So, what are we going to do this afternoon?"

"Let's go over to Leo's and just goof around," Sam suggested. "In fact," he added, glancing at Ben, "we can give old Ben here a chance to photograph something really important. Like us on blades. Unless he finds Lily more interesting of course. . . ." He smiled and pretended to study the sun, his hand cupped over his eyes.

Ben ignored him. There was no point in telling them Lily wasn't the big attraction. They'd believe what they wanted.

And so would he.

He dropped to the ground and began pulling off

his skates. Suddenly he felt a tap on his shoulder. He looked up to see Jeffers staring at him.

"Dust," Jeffers said.

Ben nodded. There seemed to be no point in discussing it further. Ever again.

11

On Monday afternoon, Ben stood unhappily in front of the giant subject index at the local library. He had never liked research, but could think of no place else to go. Not even Norm's. He needed some help. He wasn't sure he wanted it. But he definitely needed it.

Silently he ran his finger down the chest of little boxes until he came to the box marked PA–PM. He pulled it out, then grabbed a small notebook and pencil from his jacket pocket, and laid them on top of the chest. He sighed heavily and looked around the library to see if anyone was watching.

He felt like a fool. Of course, there was no one around who could have guessed why he was really there. But somehow it was still extremely embarrassing. For a moment he smiled. You ghostbuster you, he said to himself.

Ben's finger began to flick carelessly through the cards until he came to the section on photography. Slowly, one by one, he began looking for titles that might give him the information he needed.

Advances in Photography
Creative Photography
A History of Photography
Nineteenth Century Photography
Photography as Art
Portrait Photography

Ben's heart began to sink. There were more books on photography than he'd expected to find. But none of them were what he needed. Ben picked up his pencil and pad, stuffed them in his pocket, and turned away. This town is just too small. No drama, no books on photographing ghosts.

"I should have known," he muttered as he began walking toward the library's massive door. Suddenly he stopped. Ms. Horne, the librarian, was sitting at her desk, hands crossed, doing absolutely nothing. For a moment, Ben stood perfectly still, studying her.

Just at that instant she looked up, and seeing him, smiled warmly. Ben found himself walking toward her. It was as if she were a magnet.

"Can I help you, Ben?" she asked. "It's good to see you here."

For a moment, Ben was impressed she remembered him. He'd spoken to her only a few times. Then again, she was friendly with his mother.

"Ummm . . ." Ben hesitated. "Well. . . ." Ben looked down at his shoes. This is very hard, he thought to himself. She'll think I'm a maniac.

"Yes. . . ?" Ms. Horne asked again, tilting her head in an attempt to make eye contact. "How's your photography career coming along?"

Ben squared his shoulders. Do it, he said to himself. Ask her. You're here. You might as well.

"Fine." He paused. "I'd like to know if there are any books on ghosts and photography." Ben winced. He couldn't believe the way that sounded. But what was even harder to believe was the librarian's answer.

"I'm not sure there's an entire book on the subject, Ben, but I'm sure there's something about it in one or two," Ms. Horne responded with a big smile.

Ben was shocked. For a moment his mouth fell slightly open.

"Now, tell me," Ms. Horne continued, "what exactly are we talking about? Techniques, actual photographs of ghosts, or something else?"

Ben could hardly speak. She was so matter-of-fact about it. He laughed. Somehow it seemed important not to appear too serious. "I don't know," he hesitated for effect. "I guess techniques and pictures would be okay." He paused. "You know. How to. . . ."

She stood up. "Follow me."

Silently Ben followed Ms. Horne back to the card catalogue. He was about to tell her there was nothing there, when she pulled out the box marked GA–GM.

"Let's start here," she said with a smile.

He leaned over her shoulder as she began to flip.

Famous Ghosts of England
Ghostly Tales
Ghosts: Fact or Fiction?
Poltergeists
Tales of the Supernatural
White House Ghosts
World of Strange Powers

Ms. Horne stopped flipping. "There, how about that one?" she suggested.

Ben nodded quickly. He couldn't quite believe what he was doing. In fact, for a moment he wasn't even sure he wanted to do it. But he quickly wrote down the number on the card, thanked Ms. Horne, and bolted downstairs to the stacks.

Seconds later he took a corner seat at a huge

table and placed the book before him. He took a deep breath. For a moment he wished he'd told Jeffers what he was doing. He'd have liked the company. But Jeffers would have been impossible. He had no choice. Ben had to see this through on his own. Again, he looked around him, and then flipped to the back index. He began to run his second finger down the list of Ps.

It seemed to jump out at him.

Photography: Lord Combermere's Mansion, 25, Newby Church, 68, Domremy, 80

His heart began to beat wildly, and for a moment he laughed to himself. If Jeffers had been with him, he'd have had the time of his medical career.

Ben flipped to the first entry, and considered the information carefully. The year was 1891. Lord Combermere had just died when someone set up a camera in his favorite room, intending to take a simple picture. When the film was developed, there seemed to be a ghost of the late master of the house sitting in his chair. The photographer claimed no one had been in the library, though she herself had left the room during the long one-hour exposure. Nonbelievers insisted that a servant must have walked in while the camera was working, sat down in the chair, realized he was being photographed, and then quickly left. To prove the theory, it was reenacted. The results were almost identical.

Ben studied the photograph, looked up from the page and shook his head. It probably wasn't Lord Combermere, he thought to himself. He read on.

A Rev. Kenneth Lord of Newby Church in North Yorkshire in 1954 wanted to take pictures of his church. When they were developed he discovered a tall, cloaked and hooded figure with a skull-face standing near the altar. He had not seen any such figure while he was taking the picture. Everything looked completely normal through the viewfinder. He sent the film to Kodak and to an independent photographer to see if it could have been a hoax, but no one believed that to be a possibility.

Ben sat back in his chair, bringing the book up with him. A trickle of sweat began to creep down the side of his face. He studied the copy of the photograph carefully. It was terrifying. It looked like everyone's worst fantasy of a ghost. But that wasn't the thing that started another trickle of sweat on its way.

It was the simple fact that it looked like Ben's ghost. Not the shape, but the substance. It could have been dust — but it clearly wasn't. He could make out its outline, but not entirely. He could see through it, but it was definitely there. And most incredibly, the Reverend claimed not to have seen it when he took the picture. A simple picture with a simple camera. No special technique.

Ben suddenly felt very, very cold. Quickly he looked around. An old man at the other end of the table was concentrating on a huge atlas. A girl who looked like she might be a senior was flipping through two books at once, but Ben couldn't tell what they were about. Nor did he care. He was just glad she looked like a living, breathing person.

Quickly he closed his book. He had a horrible feeling that if he didn't, the ghosts would jump from the page into his life.

He stood up and walked to the stacks. Carefully he placed the book back where he'd found it, and took the stairs two at a time.

He couldn't wait to get out of the library. He had his answer. The truth was he didn't need any fancy techniques. Photographing a ghost was not up to the photographer.

It was up to the ghost.

Ben walked out into the bright sunshine and zipped his jacket. Despite the unseasonably warm temperature, he was freezing.

12

Wednesday seemed like the slowest day of Ben's life. His father was due home that evening with the contact sheets from the afternoon with Lily. He was sure he'd finally have his proof. The excitement was almost unbearable.

Ben sighed. He just couldn't shake the horrible feeling that had somehow attached itself to him . . . like a second skin. He knew what it was, too. He'd figured it out the night before. It wasn't simply the fact that he was trying to snap a picture of a ghost. That wasn't quite it. No. The real thing that was clawing at him was something else. It had to do with why. Why had that ghost started appearing before his camera? Actually lifting his arms, too. It must want something . . . something from him. And Ben didn't like that. It was one thing to focus on a ghost. It was another thing entirely for *it* to focus on you.

Ben looked down at the blank math quiz before

him. He picked up his pencil, and next to the question, "Mary has 3⅗ pounds of apples and Tom has 2⅔ pounds of apples. How many pounds of apples do they have together?" Ben drew a zero.

Who cares? he thought to himself. Mary and Tom wouldn't give a hoot about their apples if a ghost showed up.

Ben looked over his shoulder at Lily, who was now confidently filling in the answers to the quiz. It has something to do with her, he thought to himself. I hope she's okay. Guiltily he turned his eyes away. I should tell her. He shook his head.

She doesn't believe in ghosts. And besides, it could ruin everything.

"What are you doing?" a voice whispered in his ear urgently. Ben looked up just as Jeffers turned back to the quiz.

Ben looked down at his untouched paper. He had a feeling time was running out. In more ways than one.

"You are going to flunk math if you don't watch it," Jeffers offered, just as Ben took a huge bite of his hamburger. "You are also going to choke. I'd hate to have to perform a tracheotomy."

"Eh bwfat?" Ben managed as he chewed.

"A tracheotomy. It's a procedure in which someone opens up your trachea, and removes the substance that is caught, in this case rat meat from your hamburger, so that you can breathe."

Ben swallowed hard. It was often difficult to just relax around Jeffers. Medical emergencies always seemed around the corner.

"I'm not going to fail math," Ben said, grabbing a french fry from Jeffers' plate. "I just couldn't concen — "

"Hello." A familiar voice sounded in his ear. Ben looked up to see Lily standing tentatively by his table. His all *boy* table. Her tray was full, and it was clear she was looking for a place to eat.

Ben looked around the table at his friends, hoping to see at least one "sit down" smile, but there were none. Apparently his teammates had decided to keep the identity of their new coach a secret. It was too embarrassing.

Ben was about to do nothing himself, when something stopped him. She deserved more. Especially from him. Reluctantly he moved his tray over.

"So," Lily began, looking around the table with a serene smile. "I hope everyone's having a splendid day?"

No one said a word.

"Well, I hope you guys liked your skating lessons," she frowned, obviously deciding to bid Grace a quick good-bye. "I'm going to be up practicing tomorrow for the county championships at Leo's at 5 A.M." She grinned mischievously. "Any of you stars want to join me?"

That woke Sam up. "Five in the morning? I couldn't move my little toe at five in the morning."

Ben chuckled. Lily really was too much.

"Well, I can," she replied cockily. "I love skating. By the way, did you hear Leo's is closing after this week? Next week we start practicing in the sports center. The old rink is finished."

Silence descended again. Jeffers started to squirm.

"Oh," Lily continued, suddenly softening her voice, "Ben, I've been meaning to tell you. My father says the ceramics man is coming over this weekend, and I'd like some pictures of the tile going up. Can I expect you?" For a second it looked as if she was going to try and shake his hand.

Ben winced. Why did she have to ask that way? Couldn't she just say, "So, can you come?" He nodded down at his plate. What difference did it make how she said it? If she had to sound like Grace Kelly, let her. She was entitled. He had his dreams, too. The photography contest, for example.

Ben closed his eyes and tried to conjure up the

bank window. An image of his prizewinning photo began to appear. It grew closer and closer. Suddenly Ben's heart began to beat rapidly. The portrait of Lily's great-uncle was looming before him. Closer, and closer still. The sounds of the cafeteria seemed to fade away. For a strange, long moment the air felt cold. "The rope! The rope!" seemed to fill his ears, echoing almost painfully into the center of his being. Ben forced his eyes open and stared quickly at Lily.

He had to tell her. After the contest.

Ben raced home after school, and began pacing. He ate an entire bag of chocolate-chip cookies as he walked from room to room, stopping only to call his father's office three times and refuse to leave a message. He was determined to speak with him himself. He did not want to leave a reminder with his father's secretary about the film. She might forget to tell him. Like the time she neglected to remind Mr. Crisp to pick up Ben's bike at the shop. Ben never forgave her for that. He'd missed a perfect Sunday afternoon's worth of picture taking.

"You are going to feel very sick, young man, very shortly," Mrs. Crisp announced, standing in the doorway of the den. Ben looked up with surprise. He hadn't heard her come in. He had been too preoccupied. Mrs. Crisp bent down and picked up the empty cookie bag. "Is there something you'd like to talk about?" she asked, tossing it into the wastepaper basket. "You've been acting kind of funny lately." She sat down on the couch opposite Ben, and neatly folded her hands in her lap. Seconds later Stephie walked in and silently sat down next to her mother.

Ben shook his head. There was nothing he wanted to talk about. He just wanted to get things settled. Everything was too confusing to discuss.

"Well," she said with a sigh. "You know where I am if you need me." Mrs. Crisp stood up. "I love you, Ben," she added before leaving the room.

Ben smiled. She could be very nice. She just wasn't the type to listen to ghost stories. He looked at his sister. He could tell her, but she would never be objective about it. If he put a sheet over his head, and said Boo, she'd think he was a ghost. He smiled at her, too.

Stephie smiled back. She looked down at her shoes, and then up again at Ben. "Do you have any more of those pictures?" she asked quietly.

"What pictures?" Ben asked. He didn't want her getting involved. Not till he knew what was going on.

"The ghost," she replied simply. Her eyes grew wide.

"There are no ghosts, Stephie. None. Do you understand?"

Stephie smiled. "Oh, I understand all right," she said simply. "I understand lots of things. Like for instance you're too afraid to — "

Ben reached for a magazine and was about to throw it at his little sister when he heard his father's car in the driveway. He was out the front door in seconds.

13

Ben closed the door to his darkroom behind him and took a deep breath. Holding the contact sheets uncertainly in his hand, he lowered his eyes and tried to think. The blur was definitely there, just as he'd expected. It was right next to Lily in every shot.

Slowly, as if to give himself time to calm down, Ben began pouring the chemicals into separate trays. He was only slightly aware of what he was doing. He was far more aware of his growing panic.

Maybe it's not a ghost, he comforted himself. Ghosts are not real. Whatever it is only looks like a ghost. Which was fortunate. It could win him the contest, but it wasn't a ghost. No way. He'd have the camera cleaned or fixed or something — after the contest, of course. The haze would disappear and that would be that. But not before his "ghostly image" photo stole the show. He liked the title. It didn't commit him to anything. It could be, it couldn't be. That way he wasn't lying.

Ben tried to smile. There. That was the sum total of it. Now all he had to do was hope the photographs worked . . . that the odd piece of dust . . . that . . . that . . . whatever . . . would be a winner. Ben really smiled. The last few weeks he had let his imagination run away with him. But that was over now.

He glanced down at the contact sheet in his hand. It was time to develop the winning entry.

Ben turned to his enlarger. He flicked the machine on, and pulled the negatives from the envelope. He held them delicately, keeping his fingers off the film. I don't need *another* smudge, Ben thought to himself. One is enough.

Ben slipped the first negative strip into the carrier at the top of the machine, centered the light that would transpose the image onto the piece of paper, and flipped on the light switch. He could see the image on the enlarger's easel. Next he turned the wheel to enlarge the haze, and cut out the edges of the photograph. It would be important, he reasoned, to really get a close-up of the "ghost." Otherwise the judges would think he was cheating.

Turning another wheel he carefully focused the image. The results made him take a step back.

Whatever it was, it was going to be pretty clear. Ben took a deep breath. "Hang in there," he said out loud. Quickly, before he could change his mind, Ben flicked off the light, slipped a piece of hard, high contrast paper into the enlarger, and set the timer. He snapped on the enlarger light, and then he waited.

It was only for a few seconds. It felt like a year. Finally the timer went off and Ben lifted the first piece of paper off the machine. It held the shot he had taken of Lily standing next to the window. The one he'd taken moments before he'd seen the portrait.

Ben walked over to the chemical trays and placed the paper into the developer. He swished it around and around, staring down as if he were hypnotized. Ben couldn't take his eyes off the emerging image. When it was clear he swiftly placed it in the fixer and then the bath.

Then, he took the wet photograph and clipped it to the clothesline. He turned on the lights, picked up his magnifying glass, and moved closer.

Suddenly he felt as if he couldn't breathe.

The smudge was there. Or rather the man was there. In fact, now it was more man than smudge. And it was definitely Lily's great-uncle. But that was not even the thing that was terrifying. That was not what made Ben feel as if someone had

him by the chest and was squeezing . . . tighter
. . . and tighter. . . .

It was what the man was doing.

He was holding out his rope.

He was offering it to Ben.

Ben couldn't move. He wanted to. He needed
to go over to the enlarger and develop a few more
photographs. But he couldn't move. He was too
scared.

"What do you want. . . ?" Ben murmured,
clenching and unclenching his fists. "All I wanted
was a photograph to win a contest. I don't want
anything to do with you . . . or Lily. What do you
want from me? Why are you messing with my
camera?"

Ben stood silently, waiting for an answer.
Nothing happened. He looked around his
darkroom.

This is all a mistake, he told himself. Your mind
is playing tricks on you. Forget about ghosts. It's
only a trick of light or something. Like Norm
said. Submit it to the contest. Call it "A Ghostly
Image." Maybe you'll win, but stop acting nuts.
Ben nodded. Okay now. He turned to the
photograph.

Ben almost shrieked.

The man was clearer now. Practically solid.
Ben could barely make out the windowsill behind

him. There was no question about it. Lily's great-uncle wanted him to have the rope.

"I'm outta here," Ben practically shouted. "I don't want any part of this. I want to be a photographer. Not a ghostbuster." He glared at the photograph.

"Do you hear me?!" He shouted. *"I'll win that contest some other way! I don't need you!"*

In one swift motion he reached up, ripped the photograph from the line and, together with the box of negatives, threw it into the trash. He turned off the enlarger and slammed the darkroom door behind him.

Ben took the stairs two at a time, but even that didn't get him out of the basement fast enough. Photographing the ghost was one thing. Communicating with him was another. Even the contest didn't mean that much. Ben barely even noticed Stephie as he pushed past her on the way to his room.

He certainly didn't see her slowly descend the staircase to the basement.

14

Sleep," Ben instructed himself angrily. It was one in the morning and he'd been lying in bed stiff as a board for hours. "Sleep!"

He shifted positions. He turned on his right side. Then his left. He pushed the covers off. He pulled them back up to his chin. He coughed. He turned on his back.

It was no use. Ben sat up, flipped on the light, and lay back against his pillow. The facts weren't letting him sleep. Lily's great-uncle had come back from the dead. Ben's camera was proof . . . the one thing in Ben's life he could never ignore. And now the ghost was communicating with Ben.

Ben crossed his arms over his chest. The rope. Lily's uncle died because he couldn't hold on to the rope. But Lily wasn't mountain climbing. Neither was Ben, for that matter. Just taking hikes into the hills made him dizzy. So what did they need a rope for?

You don't need a rope playing hockey. A doctor, maybe. But no ropes. And figure skating could be dangerous, too, but ropes wouldn't help you there, either.

Ben shook his head. He didn't get it. He wasn't even sure he wanted to get it.

He flipped off the light, settled back into his pillow, and closed his eyes. A familiar woozy feeling began to descend. . . . Good, he said to himself . . . at last. . . .

His thoughts began to float . . . to gently wash over and around him. There he was gliding . . . floating . . . the sun beating down . . . warming him clear through his heavy jacket and thick woolen sweater. There was someone beside him. He turned. Lily. She was spinning, blonde hair whirling around her. Ben smiled. He began to skate faster . . . as if he wanted to race the cold, winter wind. Ben laughed. It felt so good. So free. He turned. Lily was still in the same spot, far away, spinning . . . spinning . . . spinning. . . . Ben laughed again. She looked so small now. He gazed up at the clear blue sky and then at the graceful pine trees. I wish I had my camera, he thought to himself, as he admired the deep green colors against the azure sky.

Ben began to glide once more, a smile on his face. He closed his eyes, and then seconds later opened them again. He was about to laugh once more . . . and then something stopped him.

It was a feeling. A bad feeling.

Ben looked up at the sky. It still looked bright blue. Maybe even brighter than moments before. And the sun, too, was still beating down. Still warming him to the core. Only Ben noticed something funny now. The sun didn't feel so comforting. In fact, he wished it would disappear. A warm breeze wrapped itself around him.

Ben broke out in a sweat. Quickly he whirled around to look for Lily. She was still twirling. He could see her bright red sweater and her fair hair spinning in the wind. But something was wrong. He couldn't quite tell what it was. He was too far away.

Ben began racing toward her, faster and faster. He could barely catch his breath. The heat was intense now. Quickly he unzipped his jacket and let it fall onto the ice. His left blade caught the zipper as the jacket slid across the frozen surface of the lake, and for a terrifying moment Ben was afraid he would trip and fall. Desperately he executed a quick turn onto his outside right blade, and with a sign of relief watched the jacket glide past and away. He turned once more and continued speeding toward Lily.

She was clearer now and Ben felt his throat

tighten. Lily was still spinning. And she was smiling. Laughing, even. She didn't see what was happening. She didn't see that she was sinking into the lake . . . that she was twirling on a piece of ice that was descending inch by inch toward the dark, gloomy, freezing bottom.

Ben began to scream. "Lily! Stop! Stop spinning!"

But she didn't stop. Faster and faster she spun. She was almost waist-deep in the lake now.

"Lily! Stop spinning! Stop spinning!"

Ben woke up with a start, sweat dripping down his cheeks. His heart pounding hard against his chest, he switched on the light and looked at the clock. It was three in the morning. Exhausted, he collapsed against his pillow.

Something awful was going to happen to Lily. He just knew it. Ben covered his face with his hands. Somehow it was up to him to stop it.

"Why me?" he asked softly. "I'm not so brave. I'm no hero. I just want to win a contest. Why me?"

He shook his head. What difference did it make, why? It was so. Period. He began to think.

How could Lily hurt herself? What could he possibly do to stop it? Ben searched his memory for a clue. She was going to skate at the old rink at five o'clock this morning. That seemed okay.

What could happen there? Of course, someone had said the place was ready to fall apart. . . .

Ben shook his head again. No. The owners of Leo's would never let her skate there if it were dangerous. And as for the lake, well, he'd just be sure to tell her not to practice there when he saw her in the morning.

Suddenly a small smile played across Ben's lips. Maybe that's all there is to this, he thought with a relieved sigh. I'm just supposed to tell Lily not to go near the lake.

Ben shut off the light and settled back more deeply into his pillows. That was it. He was sure.

But moments later Ben reached out and turned the light on once more. He set the alarm for six o'clock. He'd just take a slow walk down to the old rink and see how Lily was doing.

Why not play it safe? he thought to himself. Couldn't hurt. Maybe he'd even take his camera. Catch a few good action shots. Catch a ghost. . . .

15

"Good morning out there! Wake up, you lazy birds! Time to get up and boogie!" the voice bellowed loudly. Ben couldn't move.

"I see you! You're not fooling old Uncle Jackaroo! Get up and shake those bones!"

"No," Ben muttered into his pillow. He reached out one hand and blindly fumbled for the on/off knob of his radio alarm clock.

"It's another beautiful day, folks. That sun is going to shine —"

With a loud click the voice of Uncle Jackaroo disappeared.

Slowly Ben opened his eyes and stared at the clock. It was six o'clock. He sighed, and closed his eyes again. Just a few minutes more, he said to himself.

"*No,*" another voice from deep inside him urged. "*No. Get up.*"

Ben threw back the covers and opened his eyes.

"Right," he said out loud. He opened the door to his bedroom, and stumbled down the hall into the bathroom. Turning on the shower, he stepped inside. The warm water pounded against him and within moments he was wide awake.

I don't know why I'm doing this, he said to himself. I had one bad dream, and I'm acting like a maniac. Lily is just fine. Just fine. He let the water stream over his back. It felt good. Stepping out of the shower, he wrapped a thick towel around himself, and stared into the mirror.

"You ghostbuster you," he laughed out loud. Only inside it didn't feel so funny. He ran a comb through his hair, threw on his jeans, a flannel shirt, and his ski jacket, and headed out the door. But, when he reached the sidewalk, he suddenly doubled back. He'd forgotten his camera.

The moment he opened the door he was sorry.

"Ben, where are you going?" Stephie whispered. She was standing at the foot of the staircase completely dressed, struggling into her jacket.

"What do you think you're doing?" Ben asked irritably. The last thing he felt like doing was answering questions.

"I want to go with you," Stephie replied urgently. "I have to. I saw that picture and I had this really horrible dream and — "

"*You what?*" Ben could hardly control himself. "You went down to my darkroom? I told you never to do that! I told you. . . ."

Ben heard himself talking, but somehow the words seemed to be coming from somewhere else. It was as if his mind was divided completely in two.

"I told you never to go down there without me," he heard a voice saying.

No . . . no . . . I can't let her get involved he heard his inner self crying out.

"*Stephie!*" Ben finally grabbed her by both shoulders. "Go back to bed. *Now!* I'm just going to Leo's!"

"I don't think that's where you should. . . ."

But Ben never heard the end of her sentence. He ran to his room, grabbed his camera, and then raced out the door.

As Ben walked, his camera bouncing against his chest, he had a vague feeling that he'd forgotten something else. He hesitated. Nothing came to mind and so he quickened his step.

It was, as Uncle Jackaroo had pointed out, going to be a beautiful day. The sky was clear and bright, and as Ben walked he smiled. He unzipped his jacket, looked up at the azure sky and allowed the surprisingly warm winter wind to tickle his face. Ben felt good. It was nice being out so early in the morning . . . even if it was for a ridiculous reason.

About ten minutes later, Ben reached the old skating rink. The LEO'S FROZEN LAKE neon sign which usually flashed on and off over the entrance was now just a mass of twisting dark tubes. The place does look awful, Ben thought to himself as he drew closer to the front door. Funny how he hadn't really noticed that before. No wonder it was closing down.

He tried the door, but it was locked. He knocked, then stood back and surveyed the building. Well, it's old, he thought to himself . . . but kind of a nice landmark. He shrugged. Quickly he removed his camera from its case, took a few more steps back, and shot a picture of the entrance. Then another one just of the sign. Then he approached the door and waited. Nobody came.

Ben began to pound on the door with his fist. He couldn't figure it out. Leo's always opened early in the morning. The hockey teams from all the nearby schools practiced there. Besides, he said to himself, Lily's in there.

For a moment a tight feeling seized his stomach, but he pushed it away. "Cut it out," he said out loud. "She's fine."

Then he noticed the tiny red button next to the door. He put his finger on it and pressed for a full ten seconds. Finally he heard steps coming from inside.

"I'm comin'. I'm comin'," a muffled voice called out. "Get your finger off that darn bell."

Ben heaved a sigh of relief and stepped back. There was a rattle of keys, and then the door swung open. Ben stood face-to-face with a man who looked old enough to be someone's great-grandfather.

"What do ya want?" the man asked.

Ben peered over his shoulder, completely confused. The rink was dark. There wasn't a person on it. No hockey team. No hockey player. No Lily.

"Uh . . . uh . . ." he hesitated, trying to fight back a fierce feeling of dread. "The rink isn't open?"

"Does it look open? Does it?" the old man practically bellowed. "Yesterday was the last day. Place closed a week early. Some kind of pipe leak." He rubbed his eyes. "What is it with this town? Doesn't anybody sleep? You're the second person who's come this mornin' interruptin' my nap. No one's got any respect for the night watchman . . . no one gives a hoot about — "

"Excuse me," Ben interrupted hurriedly. "Who

110

came before me? Was it a girl with blonde hair and — "

"Yeah . . . why . . . you two lookin' to be alone here? Aren't you two a little young for. . . ."

Ben began to back away. "I'm sorry for bothering you," he said softly.

Ben turned on his heels and began to run.

She probably just went right home, he said to himself. She's probably in bed sleeping like a normal person. I'm the crazy one.

He kept running.

What am I so scared of? he kept asking himself. Why am I running? Lily's not skating. She's fine.

He was getting very hot now. He wanted to take off his jacket. Ben put one hand up to the zipper, but remembering his dream, changed his mind. He was afraid he'd trip on it.

His dream came flooding back. Spinning . . . spinning . . . spinning. . . .

Moments later Ben turned up his block. He could see the planks of new wood lying on Lily's front lawn. Drucilla's tree. One by one the houses flew by and finally he was only a few yards away from the path leading to Lily's front door. Suddenly her front door opened and Mr. Tompson stepped out.

"Well, hello, Ben," he smiled cheerfully. "You're up early. . . ."

Ben froze. He wasn't sure what to say next.

Mr. Tompson looked up at the sky. "Nice day. Unbelievably warm for this time of year, though, isn't it?"

Ben nodded. "Lily . . . Lily home?" he finally managed.

"Oh, no," Mr. Tompson smiled. "Not my girl. She's at skating practice, over at the old rink. . . ."

For a moment Ben almost told him about the camera, and the portrait, and his dream. He almost told him everything. But it seemed too impossible. Too wild. It also seemed like he couldn't have helped anyway. It was his camera . . . it was his friend . . . it was *their* ghost . . . and most importantly, he had the rope.

The rope.

That was what he had forgotten when he left the house! Ben spun around and began to race for his garage.

He had to face it now. The thing he didn't want to believe. The thing that had made him run the half mile back from Leo's, faster than he'd ever run before.

Lily was at the lake, and for some reason which he would never understand, only he and that rope could save her.

16

It was as if the rope had been waiting for him. Ben had hung it on a hook right inside the door of the garage. As the door began to open, rumbling and creaking as it rolled up into the roof, Ben reached in. With one swift movement he lifted the rope off the hook, turned, and began to run.

Overwhelmed with fear, Ben flew down the sidewalks. The lake was at least three-quarters of a mile away. It had never seemed that far before, but now it felt as if it was in another part of the world.

Ben began to sweat. It was growing more and more difficult to grasp the rope . . . which had become oddly heavy. As he ran, Ben glanced down at his burden. His eyes grew large. He couldn't be sure, but it did not look like the same rope he had hung on the garage hook a few weeks before. That one had looked dirty, but new. This one was different. The one he carried now looked old, terribly frayed — beaten up. For a moment he wondered if his father had been using the rope — or if for some reason someone had borrowed it and replaced it with another.

As he ran, Ben tried very hard to understand why the rope he was holding was unlike any other he had ever seen. Why, for some reason he was almost afraid to know, the rope looked absolutely ancient . . . or at least old enough to have belonged to a mountain climber many years before.

If it was possible, Ben ran even faster. His breath was now coming in short painful gasps. The rope had become almost unbearably heavy. Desperately he wanted to take off his jacket, but he couldn't. He would have had to stop . . . put down the rope and slip it off. There wasn't enough time. Please, Ben whispered silently. Let her be okay. She can talk like Grace Kelly every minute of the day from here on in. Just let her be okay.

Finally Ben saw the giant evergreen trees which framed the lake. He was about a block and a half away now. He couldn't be sure, but a speck of red floating to the right, and then the left seemed visible through the trees.

It's Lily, he thought to himself. It's Lily. I'm not too late.

He was bursting through the trees now. Ben opened his mouth to scream, to tell Lily to get off the ice . . . but a voice from deep inside stopped him. Don't, you'll scare her. She'll fall. The ice will surely crack then.

Quietly Ben walked to the edge of the lake, and calmly, as calmly as he could manage, he called out.

"Lily!" Ben waved. He noticed she was dangerously close to the center of the lake.

Lily whirled around, and spotting him, waved back. "What are you doing here?" she called out.

"Lily," Ben began by trying to keep his voice steady. "You have to get off the lake." His fingers began to play nervously with the rope. "The ice is too thin. . . ."

"Don't be silly," she called back. "It's fine!" She quickly did a series of backward crossovers. "Watch me!"

"No, Lily!" Ben shouted now, unable to control himself any longer. *"Stop! Get off the ice!"*

But it was too late. Lily began to execute a double axel jump and as her blade hit the ice, Ben heard it.

The unmistakable sound of ice cracking.

Lily heard it, too. Before she could complete her landing, the sound echoed over the lake. Filled with terror she whipped around to face

Ben, and a second later fell heavily onto the ice. A loud scream of pain rang through the air.

Ben watched it all with mounting horror. For endless moments it was as if the two of them were frozen in time. Neither one moved. All they could do was stare across the distance at each other's small forms.

Suddenly Ben felt the rope literally shaking in his hand. Terrified he would look to his right and find Lily's great-uncle trying to wrest it from his grasp, he refused to turn. Seconds later he realized his entire body was shaking. It was he, not the ghost, who was making his arm tremble.

He looked down at the rope and out at Lily, who was still so frozen with fear she could do nothing but stare in his direction, and the huge crack that now led from her to the side of the lake, branching out into many more smaller fissures in the ice.

Ben looked down at the rope. As if it would speak to him. But he was lost. He could not figure out what he was supposed to do with it. He couldn't throw it to her. She was too far away. He couldn't bring it to her. He weighed more than she did.

"Lily," he called out. "Stay flat. Try and move very carefully toward me!"

"I can't!" she cried back. "I can't. I think I

broke my ankle! I can't move. It hurts too much!" Ben could hear her sobs as clearly as if she were standing beside him.

He began to look around the clearing, desperately hoping a solution would appear . . . some clue to what he was supposed to do. Tears began to well up in his eyes. I should have told Lily's father, he repeated to himself over and over. I should have told Lily about the ghost. A tear began to trickle down his cheek. He bent down and picked up a large rock. Maybe I should tie the rope to this and send it gliding toward her, he thought to himself. It'll never work, another voice said. Never.

Ben was just about to tell Lily to lay perfectly still and wait for him to come back with help, when he heard the sound of soft steps behind him. Overwhelmed with relief he whirled around.

Stephie was standing in the clearing, a few feet away.

"Oh, no!" Ben cried out softly, a sob catching in his throat. "What are you doing here?" he whispered, as if he were afraid his voice would crack the ice further.

Stephie came up and stood close beside him. "I had this terrible dream last night about Lily and . . . and. . . ." She looked out over the lake. "I tried to tell you." She gripped his arm tightly.

Ben looked away, trying to fight his own tears. He'd heard her say that earlier, but he'd wanted to ignore it. The thought was too incredible. But now, somehow, seeing the three of them together, everything was becoming clear. This was what the ghost had feared. He was trying to protect Lily through Ben. He'd even reached out to Stephie, just to be sure. And now, because Ben hadn't let on because of the contest, the world felt as if it were coming apart.

"I . . . I'm going for help," Ben said shakily. "Stay here. Tell her not to move. . . ." He began to move toward the trees.

"Ben! Don't leave me! What if the ice gets worse? Look! It already is!" Tearfully, Stephie pointed at the lake.

Ben looked. She was right. The ice was beginning to look like an uneven spiderweb of cracks. Lily was trapped. She needed help *now*.

Ben looked at his sister. "I have to get her the rope."

Stephie, walking delicately as if the frozen ground itself were the thin ice of the lake, approached the edge. For a few moments she studied Lily, who was lying completely still on the lake surface. She turned to Ben.

"What are we going to do?" she sobbed. Her shoulders were shaking.

118

Ben had no idea. "I don't know. I've got to get this rope to her — only *I* can't do it. There's no one to pull me in and one false move and I'd cave the ice in for sure."

Stephie stared intently out over the lake. "But not me . . ." she murmured softly. Stephie had suddenly stopped crying. "I could go. . . ."

"Oh, no. No way," Ben countered. "I'm not sending you out there. I'd sooner go myself." He placed his hand gently on her shoulder.

"Ben," Stephie replied, eyes glued to Lily. "I can do it. . . ."

Ben was about to repeat his protest, when he heard another horrifying sound — like a crackling fire. He whipped around almost afraid to look, but saw with great relief that it was only a large branch that had fallen from a nearby tree. He peered up at the sky. The sun was still low and shining brightly. He could tell it was going to be another warm day. The ice wouldn't hold out much longer. He had to make a decision.

He turned and studied his sister for a long moment. He was faintly aware that his mind had gone completely blank. It was as if he needed to step away from the pressure. Just for a moment.

She really does have beautiful blue eyes, Ben said to himself. He had a sudden impulse to hug her very hard, but something inside suddenly pulled him back to the lake. "Okay," he said softly. He could hear his heart pounding. *What have I done?* a voice inside him whispered. First Lily, now Stephie. *What have I done?*

He looked down at the rope and took a deep breath. "I'm going to tie this rope around your waist, and then I want you to get on your stomach and slide very slowly across the ice. When you reach Lily, take both her hands in yours and don't let go. I'll pull you both back. But *stay on your stomach.*"

Stephie looked out over the ice uncertainly, then back at Ben. "B . . . But Ben, you're not all that strong. How are you going to do that?"

"The ice will make it easy," he replied, not at all sure that was true. Stephie was right. He wasn't very strong. "Besides," he added, glancing at a big stump that stood to their left. I'm going to tie one end to this stump. That will help a lot. Each time I pull you in a little further I'll wind the rope around the tree and knot it, so if I have to let go you'll stay put."

Stephie was about to answer when Lily called out in a frightened voice, "What are you waiting for? *Do something!*"

Stephie looked out over the lake and gently rested her hand on the rope. "Okay. Let's go!"

Quickly Ben tied one end of the rope around

his sister, and the other end around the stump. "Remember," he said to her firmly, "the whole way on your stomach! Go slow! If you see or hear any ice cracking under you I want you to tell me. If I say I'm pulling you back, lie very still, and I'll do the work." Ben took a deep breath, and then got to the hard part. "If, after you are holding onto Lily I tell you to let go of her, do it."

Ben didn't mention his worst fear . . . that Stephie would let go, and Lily wouldn't. That they'd both go crashing through the ice and it would all be over.

Stephie nodded quickly. Moments later she was lying flat on the ice slowly making her way toward Lily, who could now be heard sobbing with fear in the dead center of the lake.

17

Ben's hands were beginning to hurt. The rope was coarse and the tiny fibers were tearing into his skin. He did not relax his grip. Stephie was only a quarter of the way over to Lily. It would be a long time before he could allow himself to release his fierce hold.

The sun was now shining steadily in the sky. Ben twisted his wrist slightly to check his watch. It was seven o'clock exactly. His parents would be getting up soon. In about fifteen minutes they would probably notice he and his sister were gone.

Ben grimaced. In fifteen minutes it would be history. He would have either succeeded or fa —

"Ben! Ben!" Stephie's high-pitched voice pierced the air. "I hear something . . . *listen!*"

Ben squinted against the sun. It was difficult to stare at the ice. The glare was intense. "Don't move, Steph," he called out, desperately trying to locate any new threatening cracks. He could see nothing.

He released another two feet of rope and tightened his grip. "Stephie. I can't see any new cracks. Can you?"

He saw her carefully turn her head from right to left. "No!" she called back.

Ben felt a sudden cramp threaten to overpower his left hand. He relaxed his grip for a moment, and flexed his fingers. Then he took hold of the rope once more. He hesitated. "Okay. Keep moving Steph. Slowly. . . ."

Ben leaned forward, trying to make out the condition of the ice, and for the second time that morning he remembered his camera. It swung against him gently as his upper body moved forward.

He looked down at it for a moment, and then back again at Stephie. She was now almost halfway to Lily, who was lying perfectly still, her eyes trained on his little sister.

Ben looked down at his camera again and then suddenly, for a moment, closed his eyes. He could not believe what he was thinking.

The contest. The drama.

His eyes flew open. *No*, a voice from deep inside him screamed. NO! How could you? Look at what's happening out there! What's the matter with you? Guiltily, Ben squinted against the sun. Stephie was moving steadily now. She was very brave. He released another few feet of rope, and for a moment let go with one hand and held it up to shield his eyes. The ice was holding. So far so good.

"Looking good, Steph . . ." he called out encouragingly. She kept moving. She was close to Lily now. Their eyes were trained on each other. It was as if they were locked in a frightening little world all their own . . . as if he didn't exist . . . as if it didn't much matter what he did.

A *drama* unfolding before him. . . .

Ben glanced down one more time at his camera. It swung temptingly against him. Almost teasing him.

He looked back at Stephie. She looked fine. Everything would be okay. He was growing more and more sure of it. The ice was probably thicker than he'd thought. If he let go of the rope for just a moment or two, tying it securely around the tree stump of course, just long enough to take a shot, maybe even two — everyone would still be okay. It was now or never. Pretty soon there'd be no way. . . .

He began to loosen one hand on the rope. Slowly his fingers relaxed and began to edge toward the camera case.

"Just one shot," Ben muttered. "Just one. Maybe two. . . ."

His fingers began to fumble with the case buckle. It was difficult to undo. His hand was badly cramped from hanging onto the rope so tightly. Finally he released the clasp and began to flip up the top of the case.

And then something clicked.

Ben didn't know what it was. Thinking back on it later that night he was still unsure of what he'd heard. It could have been another ice crack, a twig, the wind through the trees, the change in his pockets, or just a feeling deep inside himself that suddenly leaped forward demanding to be heard.

It might even have been a force from another world making sure he did what he had to do. . . .

But it was enough.

Ben's right hand flew back to the rope. And at that instant, another resounding crack echoed across the lake.

Several yards to the right of the girls, who were now almost touching, Ben saw a slow gush of freezing water coming from a fresh, large, threatening crack. He had to fight the urge to quickly pull Stephie back to safety.

Don't Ben, he told himself. Don't. Just a few more seconds and Stephie will have Lily.

And moments later he was right.

"I've got her!" Stephie called back. It sounded as if she were whispering. Ben could barely hear her. She hadn't dared turn her head.

"Good!" Ben yelled back. "Good! Hold onto her tight!"

"I hope you know what you're doing!" Lily cried out.

"*I do!*" Ben replied, not wanting to tell her the truth — that he was terrified. More terrified than he'd ever been in his whole life. And that it felt as if the strength in his arms were about to give out.

Slowly he began to pull in the rope. It was harder than he had expected. Somehow he'd imagined that the slippery ice would give him little resistance. But getting the two girls moving was near to impossible.

For a moment Ben stopped and tried to think. He looked around, but could find nothing or no one to help. Looking back at the two girls, he again tightened his grip.

"We have to help," Lily called back, her voice sounding weak and unsure. He could barely hear her. "We're going to push." She was silent for a moment. Ben could tell she was talking with Stephie. Then she called out again, louder this time. "I'm going to hold the rope with one hand and push off with the other." She said something else

126

but Ben couldn't quite make it out. He stood perfectly still, straining to hear. "Listen!" she tried again. He could hear her panic. "Rope! Send more rope so I can wind it around my hand!" Lily cried out desperately. He knew she was screaming but the wind had picked up ever so slightly and her voice sounded like the tiniest whisper.

Ben was about to do as she asked when a loud crackle filled the air, and a flow of icy water began to bubble to the surface inches away from Stephie and Lily. Any moment, he knew, it would be seeping into their clothing, chilling them mercilessly.

"The rope! The rope!" Lily screamed. It seemed to echo deep and strong across the lake. It seemed to fill the trees, the sky . . . Ben's mind.

The next instant she grabbed the slack that had appeared beside Stephie, and with their faltering help Ben began, with all his might, to pull them in. The water was gushing heavily through the crack, and for one horrifying moment it appeared that Lily and Stephie were afloat on a giant island of ice — about to be swallowed up by the dark, freezing deep of the lake.

But seconds later, slowly and carefully, they began to inch away from the hungry split.

Ben pulled hard, winding the rope around the

tree stump for added support. Every muscle in his body strained to pull the girls to safety. They were now able to help, as they gently pushed off the icy surface with their legs and hands. His mind blocked out everything, everything except the sudden and strange sensation that he was not alone. That there was someone beside him helping. Pulling . . . pulling . . . pulling. . . .

About a minute later both girls were clear of the treacherous center. And only then did Ben allow himself to realize what he had heard.

"The rope! The rope!" echoed in his ears. The cries of a desperate man long gone. . . .

18

I told you," Jeffers shook his head with disgust. "I told you. . . ."

Ben couldn't believe it. Slowly he lowered himself into a cold metal chair in his darkroom and gently placed the magnifying glass down on the counter. Stephie picked it up and held it over the photograph. She stared silently.

"There are no such things as ghosts," Jeffers intoned. "Say it Ben. There are no such things as ghosts."

"B . . . But . . . how did I know? How did I know to go to the lake? That I needed the rope?" Ben reached up and pulled at Jeffers' sleeve in frustration. "Tell me that!"

"Coincidence, my boy," Jeffers replied. "Yesterday was a big coincidence. And if you try to explain it any other way to your damsel in distress, she's going to think your marbles went for a walk without you."

"What about the rope? It wasn't the same. It was different! Old! And where is it now?" Ben cried out in frustration. He'd gone back that afternoon to the lake but the rope had completely disappeared.

"Someone walked off with it," Jeffers answered casually. "People take things, Ben. They find things, pick them up, decide they like them, and then take them. That's what people do."

Ben's head was spinning now. He looked back at the photographs he had pulled from the garbage. He closed his eyes and opened them again as if somehow that would change things. But it didn't.

The ghostly haze was hardly visible now. He threw the photographs back into the trash.

"I mean, honestly, Ben," Jeffers continued, slipping his jacket off the back of the chair. "Keep this thing to yourself, okay? You can trust me. I'm not going to call the funny farm. But Lily might. It was a good move — not telling her first thing and all. Just let her keep thinking you and Steph were out for a walk." Jeffers pulled up his zipper and looked at Stephie with concern. "You'll keep your mouth shut, right? Not that anyone would believe you."

Stephie placed both hands on her small hips

indignantly. "My friends always believe me, Jeffers."

Ben nodded warmly at his sister. "Better keep your mouth shut anyway, Steph. I mean," he paused, waving his hand around the darkroom with disgust, "where's the proof?" Then he covered his face with his hands and tried to think. Could he really have made the whole thing up? He couldn't believe that. Not even the contest could have made him fool himself that much. Or could it have?

Suddenly Ben slumped further into his chair. The contest. He'd actually not even thought about it for an entire day.

"What are you doing?" Jeffers asked, one hand resting on the darkroom door. "You okay? Maybe you should let me take a look at you. . . ." He began unzipping his jacket. "Maybe your glands are swollen, or —"

"No! No!" Ben waved him away. "Enough. I need to think. That's all. . . . Go. Please." He started to reach for the photographs.

"Oh, no," Jeffers argued, pulling on Ben's arm. "No more. Leave that picture in the garbage and let's get outta here. And I mean now."

Ben sighed. "Maybe you're right. Enough is enough." He allowed himself to be pulled to his feet. "I guess I just have to forget about it. I guess I just have to pretend this never happened." He turned to his sister. "You, too," he added irritably. "In fact, this whole thing might not have gotten started if you hadn't been so gassed up about ghosts to begin with!" He settled a glare on his sister. "You better pretend this never happened."

Instantly Ben felt horrible. He started to place his hands gently on Stephie's shoulders, but she had already backed away, a look of betrayal on her face.

"No, Ben," Jeffers said. "She doesn't have to pretend anything. Nothing happened. There are no ghosts. *No ghosts.*"

He whirled around to face Stephie. "Enough!" Jeffers proclaimed, one finger pointing to the door.

"Don't tell me what to do," Stephie replied defiantly, though it was clear Jeffers' tone had shaken her. "I know a ghost when I see one." She began backing away and moments later she sprinted from the room.

"Hey, Jeffers . . ." Ben started to protest, but Jeffers was already pulling him toward the door.

"Say good-bye," Jeffers insisted. "I don't think you ought to come down here for a while."

Ben turned and looked around the room for only a moment, and then switched off the light.

But he didn't say good-bye.

"There you are!" Mrs. Crisp practically sang out as the two boys wandered into the den. "The phone has been ringing off the hook for you and Stephie! Even the mayor called!"

Suddenly Mr. Crisp jumped from his seat and folded Ben into his arms. "You're quite a guy, Ben. Quite a guy."

"I'm not," Ben said, struggling out of his father's grasp.

"You are," Jeffers said, throwing himself down on a comfortable easy chair.

"Here," Mrs. Crisp went on, handing Ben a number on a piece of paper. "Call the editor of the *Windsor News*. They want to interview you and Stephie."

Ben looked down at the number and shrugged. "Maybe Stephie should. . . ."

"*You call.*" Jeffer's voice seemed to fill the room.

Ben whipped around to face his friend. "Okay. I will. And what story should I tell? Huh? What?" His eyes darted around the room in wild confusion.

"What are you talking about, Ben?" Mrs. Crisp asked. She glanced at Jeffers with a look of bewilderment.

"I haven't a ghost of an idea," Jeffers said shaking his head, his eyes not leaving Ben's. "Not a ghost." He started chuckling.

For a moment Ben considered punching his best friend in the gut. But instead he took a deep breath, stuck his hands in his pockets, and smiled.

"Yuk, yuk," he said softly as his fingers wound tightly around the editor's number.

19

Ben stood outside the new Westmore Sports Arena clutching his skates in one hand. He looked up with awe at the new superstructure. It was the biggest building he'd ever seen in his life. He couldn't imagine how far away he'd have to stand in order to capture the entire thing in one frame. He'd need a helicopter.

Instinctively his hand went to his chest, but the camera wasn't there. A feeling of sadness clutched his heart. For the last two weeks he'd taken to leaving it home. On purpose. His interest in the photography contest had almost completely disappeared.

"Ready?" a voice from behind him sang out. Jeffers thumped Ben's back hard. "How's it going, you hero, you?"

"Okay," Ben answered with impatience. "Enough." Quickly he looked away. At first it had been fun. The whole town had treated him and

Stephie like they deserved the key to city hall for saving Lily. As if he were the bravest kid in the world. And for a while he'd gotten himself to believe that. But it was getting harder and harder. There were too many unanswered questions. Like, who really saved Lily? Him or the ghost? And could he have stopped the whole thing from happening if he'd told Lily what he suspected in the first place? So what if she laughed or ruined his chances at the contest?

Jeffers shook his head. "Look Ben, you know I'm a scientist. I like things concrete. Here it is. I've figured the whole mess out. You had a bad dream. Maybe somewhere you overheard Leo's was closing early, but you didn't consciously remember. In other words, you forgot. Then, in your sleep you put two and two together. Lily wouldn't be able to skate at Leo's like she'd said, and the only other place she could go was the lake. You knew that was dangerous so you had a dream that kind of warned you." He paused and smiled, extremely pleased with himself. "The unconscious mind is capable of many things," he added.

"But . . ." Ben began to protest.

"But nothing!" Jeffers cried out in exasperation. "So you thought you were seeing ghosts. Big deal. You still saved her." He thumped Ben's back again. "Feel good about it, would you? I wish I'd saved her. I'd love everyone to think I'm a hero." To underline his point, Jeffers began to wave to his invisible admirers. "Thank you," he called out solemnly. "Yes. I am an incredible person. Thank you."

Ben watched him for a moment and then began to laugh. "Maybe you're right," he said slowly. It was true. What difference did it make what drove him to the lake? Even if he'd told Lily about the ghost she might still have been out skating. It wasn't as if the ghost had ever actually told Ben what could happen. No. It was his challenge. His victory. A big, broad smile began to play across his lips. He, Ben Crisp, had saved Lily. Ghost or no ghost. He was definitely a hero. Sort of.

Ben looked at the admirers to whom Jeffers was still waving, and raised his own hand. "Please . . . please . . ." he proclaimed loudly. "It was nothing. No clapping." Ben felt a rush of good feeling. "I did what a man has to do," he added.

And with that he and Jeffers walked into Westmore, imagined applause ringing in Ben's ears.

Silently they took the escalator up to the top floor and headed for the huge double doors that opened onto the skating rink. The sounds of applause grew louder. Only this time it was for real.

"Okay. Enough!" Lily was calling out, as Ben

and Jeffers walked into the brightly lit arena. She was laughing at the rest of the Snow Kings who were standing around the rink clapping loudly. "This is your last skating lesson before your game with the Ice Hawks. The show is over. My ankle can't take any more today." She clapped her hands. "Gentlemen! Ice please!"

Ben burst out laughing. It was unbelievable. Even when she turned Grace on, she was beginning to sound normal. Nice, too.

"Okay, Coach!" Sam cried out, as he whizzed onto the ice enthusiastically. Moments later he was lying facedown.

"Wow, Sam," James called out. "Nice move. Too bad your skates don't fit your head!"

Ben was just about to add "or your nose" when he spotted Stephie. She was standing in the corner of the arena, watching.

Guiltily, he walked over to her. Since the incident in the darkroom Ben had managed to avoid any big conversations with Stephie. He'd been afraid she'd start in again with too many questions. Questions that would make him lie awake every night . . . instead of every other night. All he wanted was to put the ghost thing behind him. Be a hero. That's all.

"What's up?" he said when he reached her side. "What are you doing here?"

Stephie shrugged, staring past him with annoyance. "Lily's going to give me lessons when you're through. That's all."

Ben nodded. "That's very nice of her."

Stephie peered at him curiously. "I was at the lake, too, you know," she said simply. "I saved her, too."

Ben stared into her not-so-innocent, big blue eyes. "I know that," he said. "You were terrific." Suddenly it occurred to him she might have thought he was ignoring her, so he could soak up all of the applause.

"I tell everyone how unbelievable you were," Ben volunteered with a big smile. "How brave and everything."

"Really?" Stephie commented with a trace of annoyance. "Tell them anything else?"

Ben turned away. He didn't want to think about it. Part of him just wanted to forget he'd been there himself. In his darkroom, in Lily's house, behind the camera lens, at the lake.

With a grim expression on his face, Ben walked back to his teammates. He could feel his sister's eyes upon him. Urging him to face the truth . . . whatever that might be. Letting him know that neither of them could put it to rest until. . . .

But moments later his dark mood was broken.

Max skated into the center of the ice, and

promptly executed a very fast scratch spin. Ben figured he must have completed five full turns.

"Hey, Max?" Jeffers called out. "You think that's going to give us a win next Saturday? Last time I watched the Flyers they didn't seem too interested in spins." Everyone began to laugh.

"Maybe you'd like a little skating skirt?" James shouted. "I'm sure we'd all be happy to — "

"For your information," Lily interrupted him sternly, "male figure skaters wear pants not unlike the ones you have on." She pointed to his bright red sweats. "Besides, if you could put aside your macho garbage it would do you good to learn a scratch spin. It'll give you control over the ice." She flashed James a sweet smile and then turned to face the others.

Max grinned triumphantly, and executed another perfect scratch spin.

Moments later, with Lily in the center of the ice, the Snow Kings began to warm up, skating smoothly and quickly around the perimeter of the rink.

Ben took deep, measured breaths as he moved. He felt good. Really good. Better than he had since . . . since looking at that picture of Lily as she walked away from him. The picture that had started the whole nightmare.

Ben looked over his shoulder at Lily, as she

shouted out suggestions. For a moment he remembered almost letting go of the rope. He shuddered. Visions of the haze that had hovered next to Lily began to float before his eyes.

It was a ghost. It wasn't a ghost. It was a ghost. It wasn't a ghost. Over and over the words danced inside his head. Ben looked up at the floodlit ceiling helplessly.

Soon, Ben promised himself. Soon I will know for sure. It will drive me crazy if I don't. I can't just forget about it. I have to know for sure.

But for the life of him, Ben couldn't figure out how he ever would.

"Ben! Where are you?" Lily suddenly called out. "Concentrate!"

"Okay! Okay!" Ben called back with mock annoyance. He shot her a big smile, suddenly overwhelmed with the desire to do something really nice for her . . . something special only he could do.

Something with no uninvited guests.

20

W hat do you think?" Jeffers said, staring over Ben's shoulder.

"I don't know yet," Ben replied, gingerly lifting the photograph out of the fixer. He let it drip for a moment over the tub of chemicals and then clipped it to the clothesline. He snapped on the light.

He had caught her perfectly. Ben smiled triumphantly. "I did it," he proclaimed.

Jeffers leaned in. "You're good. That's a fact."

Lily studied the photograph. "I'm good. That's a fact."

The three of them silently stared down at the dramatic photograph of Lily. She was midair, moments away from landing a perfect, elegant jump. Her hair streamed gracefully around her face, her arms rested close to her body, and her legs remained straight in perfect position. Behind her the trees surrounding the lake seemed to under-line her flight . . . almost to hold her aloft.

Three weeks before, the weather had suddenly gone below freezing.

"Well," Jeffers announced, "it's beyond me how your twisted ankle healed so well in just one month, but the truth is I gotta go." He settled a serious look on Lily. "Are you sure you don't want me to take a look at that ankle?" He started to bend down.

Instantly Lily backed away. "No, thanks," she said quickly. "It wasn't a bad sprain."

Jeffers shrugged and turned back to Ben. "Good luck with the contest. You bringing this over to the bank today?"

Ben nodded. "You bet," he hesitated for a moment. "You two go ahead. I'm going to clean up." Ben looked around him. Things looked awfully dusty. He hadn't been down there since the day after the accident. Even now he still felt a little uncomfortable.

"Umm, well, thanks, Ben," Lily said sincerely. "This will be a great publicity shot." She paused for a moment, peering down at the photograph. "Do . . . do . . . you think I look a little like Grace Kelly here . . . well . . . not quite *like* her . . . but you know . . . her *style*. . . ."

Ben sighed. He couldn't say yes and he couldn't say no, though he'd have liked to tell Lily what she wanted to hear. He still wasn't sure he'd ever seen Grace Kelly.

"A little . . ." Jeffers suddenly piped up, smiling at Lily. He turned to Ben. "You know, she's in this great Hitchcock movie called *Rear Window*. Have you ever seen it? You'd love it. It's about this photographer who witnesses this murder and. . . ."

"I know, I heard," Ben interrupted him with surprise. "Since when are you a Grace Kelly fan?"

"I'm not," Jeffers laughed. "I just like scary movies." He looked at his watch again. "Gotta go."

"Actually, mind if I just stick around for a second?" Lily asked, letting her eyes travel around the darkroom. "It's kind of spooky down here. But nice."

"It's okay," Ben said reluctantly. He had a few things he wanted to check out on his own. "But I have to work."

"Well, see you later," Jeffers picked up his books and started out the door. Then he turned to Lily. "Don't forget about James. He's probably practicing right now." And with that the door closed behind him.

Ben looked at Lily curiously. "What's that all about?"

Lily chuckled. "Oh, James is having trouble with his turns on the ice. That's the reason his hockey game is so bad. I'm giving him extra lessons."

She rested her fingertips on the enlarger. "What's this?" she asked. "It's bizarre-looking."

"Just a piece of developing equipment," Ben answered quickly. It just wouldn't stop haunting him . . . the fact that he hadn't told her. After all, it was her great-uncle. Of course, maybe it *wasn't* her great-uncle. Maybe it was just her cold breath. He shot a quick glance at Lily. Could he possibly tell her the whole story? It wasn't hard to imagine what she'd say if she knew he'd almost let go of the rope.

"Listen, Ben," Lily's voice suddenly became serious, "I don't think I ever did thank you enough for saving me like that." She kept her eyes on the enlarger. "You really were very brave."

Ben couldn't look at her. It was just too much. All month he'd been half expecting a congratulatory phone call from the White House.

"In the beginning I really thought you were just a selfish pain in the neck. But you're really not and I. . . ."

That was it.

"You don't understand," Ben began slowly.

"It's not that I'm so brave. So good. I should have told you. I'm impossible. I never should have. . . ."

Lily started to laugh. "Oh, I get it. You should have left me out there." She sighed. "Well, I guess you have to keep that act up." Suddenly Lily turned from the enlarger, threw one arm around Ben's neck, and planted a kiss on his cheek.

"You're okay, Ben Crisp," she proclaimed. "And now I really must go. My student needs me."

And with that she sailed out the door.

"What? No handshakes?" Ben called after her, pretending to be annoyed. He smiled sadly down at his shoes. Maybe she just wasn't meant to know.

Ben listened as Lily climbed the stairs, and waited for the door to the basement to click shut. He looked around his darkroom and took a deep breath. Then, slowly, as if to give himself time to change his mind at each step, he reached into the tabletop drawer and pulled out a magnifying glass. He took another deep breath and finally trained it on the spaces on either side of Lily in the photograph.

Nothing. He'd thought so. The contact sheet hadn't shown anything, either. He felt his heartbeat slow down. He lowered his head with a mixture of relief and disappointment.

The wastepaper basket came into focus. Ben leaned down and carefully picked out the picture that had saved Lily's life . . . and almost ruined his own. The one with the rope.

He pinned it to the clothesline and once again picked up his magnifying glass.

The haze. It was still there. Ben studied it carefully for about a minute and then gently placed the magnifying glass down on the counter.

Somehow he wasn't sure anymore. It looked like a haze. If he stretched his imagination very far he could see the man. But not as clearly now. Not as clearly as he had a little over a month before.

Dust, he thought to himself. Could all of this have been just a matter of dust? He shook his head. If only he had the rope. Ben began to dump the chemicals out into the sink. What really happened? he asked himself over and over. No matter how hard he tried he couldn't sort through the facts . . . if there even were any. Finished, he hesitated for just a second and then went back to the counter and lifted the magnifying glass once more.

He studied the haze next to Lily. "It could be a ghost," he said out loud. "It could be. . . ." Visions of winning the blue ribbon for best dramatic photograph whizzed through his head.

But somehow it didn't seem right. If it was Lily's great-uncle, he'd appeared for only one reason. A really important reason. Ben couldn't use that.

Or could he?

Ben lowered the magnifying glass and focused on the photograph of Lily in midflight.

"I can't," he said finally. Ben quickly glanced at the other picture as if to say, "Okay? That's it, then."

Only it wasn't.

For a long moment Ben stared in shocked silence. The magnifying glass fell from his grasp and clattered onto the table.

The haze had completely disappeared.

But in its place, once again, stood the clear and powerful image of Lily's great-uncle. He seemed to be talking to Ben. Reaching out. Almost smiling.

Only this time he wasn't holding a thing. In fact there was no rope in the photograph at all. This time he was merely extending his hand. As if to say thank you.

For a moment Ben closed his eyes. "This can't be happening," he murmured. Desperately he wished someone were there with him. Even Stephie. Someone to be a witness. Someone to tell him he wasn't crazy. He opened his eyes and looked again.

Lily's great-uncle was gone.

A sharp pain ripped through Ben's stomach. "Stop teasing me," he cried out softly. "Stop appearing and disappearing. It isn't fair. I did what I could." He reached out and touched the spot where Lily's uncle had appeared. "The truth, please," he pleaded. "Were you really here?"

Ben's hands began to shake. He gripped the table in front of him as fiercely as he had the rope that day at the lake. Again, his hands began to ache.

And then suddenly, almost magically, Ben knew. The thought wrapped itself around him gently, warming him like a soft, thick, woolen blanket. A smile began to play across his lips.

A moment later Ben turned, and without looking back he walked out of the darkroom and closed the door behind him with a soft click. He climbed the stairs very slowly and headed for his sister's room.

I did it, he thought. I did the one thing Lily's great-uncle couldn't do for himself or Lily. Ghost or no ghost. It was me. I, Ben Crisp, didn't let go. Despite my camera. Despite the most important contest of my life. I held onto the rope.

Ben's smile widened with pride. Reaching his sister's door he was about to raise his hand to knock, when it suddenly swung open.

Stephie stood facing him with the oddest expression he'd ever seen on anyone in his whole life.

"What's up?" he asked, momentarily putting aside why he had come. She looked almost excited. But not quite.

Slowly Stephie lowered her eyes. Ben followed her glance and for a very long moment he stared in thoughtful silence.

In Stephie's small hand, dangling limply onto the floor, was the rope.

"It just appeared in my room a few minutes ago," Stephie started to babble. "I mean, I *think* it just appeared. I found it under my bed. You didn't put it there, did you? Maybe Dad did. Or Mom." She paused a second, and then stepped back as if to put some safe distance between herself and her brother. "I know you don't believe in . . . but don't you think it's possible that. . . . " Stephie let her voice trail off. She took another step backward. "Don't yell at me," she added.

But Ben had no intention of doing that.

Tentatively he reached out and let his fingertips rest lightly on the frayed rope found in Stephie's room.

"I think he just said thank you to both of us," Ben said evenly.

"He did?!" Stephie said, clasping both her hands together with pleasure. The rope fell to the floor.

"He did," Ben said, surer than he'd been about anything for a long time.

Suddenly Stephie's face clouded over. "But maybe Mom or Dad put. . . ."

Ben started to laugh. "You, of all people! I cannot believe this! The original Ms. Ghost of the Year!"

For a moment Stephie hesitated and then she, too, began to laugh. Bending down, Ben gripped the rope tightly in his hand, and made a mental note not to check with his parents. It simply didn't matter one little bit.

About the Author

Meg Schneider lives in Irvington, New York, with her husband and small son. She has written many nonfiction books for young readers. Meg is not sure if she believes in ghosts, but she is absolutely positive it is a decision each person has to make for themselves.

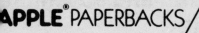